THE GOLDEN LINE

ADDISON CAIN

1

———

hey were coming.

Gaping like a fish, Morgaine fell from sleep into agony. Wide eyes locked on the rugged ceiling beams above her cot. She couldn't breathe. A great invisible force pressed down against her ribs, the unseen weight of a full-grown man crouching on her chest as if to tell her, *stay*.

Tongue tracing dry lips, she closed her eyes, counted to ten, and scrounged up the will to force her lungs to expand, contract, and expand again. Next, she worked to uncurl her cramping fingers—knowing it wouldn't be long before they grew gnarled, muscles winding tight until each digit locked into place.

Waking in such misery could only signify one thing.

She didn't have much time.

Morgaine had to hide. She had to get out of her bed, ignore the spreading fire shooting through each nerve, and find a place to suffer alone before *they* found her.

The horrors that haunted her dreams every eve of *their* arrival were nothing. The pain clawing through sinew and bones the closer *they* came was nothing. The feeling of being hunted, of hairs rising on the back of her neck, didn't matter.

The deep-seated shame for what would happen should the hated ones find her... *mattered greatly*.

Morgaine would rather die. She could never abide their eyes on her, their hands.

Alphas...

Alphas approached. Close enough now that she couldn't waste a precious second.

Season after season they infected her settlement—to look over their chattel, to drag away friends and loved ones who were never seen again. All colonists understood survival required a show of respect to the *ruling* invaders.

Never look them in the eye.

Should a foreign soldier approach, settlers were expected to go to their knees and prostrate themselves for inspection.

Never speak unless spoken to.

Those who argued, who fought... they were made examples of.

Morgaine had seen unspeakable things: whippings, brandings, executions.

They took whomever they wished. Older children, younger men and women—those the settlement needed *most*. They tore families apart. Pleading screams were a common song on the days the Alphas came to take.

Some even grew numb to it. Some looked away.

Others, like her, spent their years plagued by nightmares and regret. You could hear it in the settlement after dark, the hum of sad moans, the creak of neighbors tossing and turning as sweat soaked through their threadbare sheets.

Everyone carried the stain.

Her personal hell was the undying memory of her older cousin—how hard he had fought when massive soldiers seized him. She had been a frightened child of eight. The boy, her hero, had been only thirteen.

The last time she saw him he was calling for his mother, blood dribbling from a split lip. It took two of the soldiers to cart him away.

Morgaine's aunt had been held down by her own people when she'd tried to intervene. The settlers had not done it to be cruel. They had done it to save her life.

Endless, awful months followed where her aunt wept for her stolen son. No amount of *reimbursement* had eased the woman's despair. What was money when one's only child was gone? When she knew she would never see him again?

If the Alphas marked you, there was no return. Ever.

No one knew what became of those they took, and any who dared to ask were silenced. Her aunt had been unable to hold her tongue the next season the Alpha invaders returned. Begging for news, the woman had run to the first soldier she'd found. He threw her off. She scrambled to another. As the story goes, it was the fifth, less patient brute who'd hacked out her tongue.

No son, no way to communicate… it was less than a year before she took her own life.

Morgaine would never let such suffering befall her mother. And there was one sure way to prevent it— she'd not let the beasts set eyes upon her since that morning they'd found her mother's sister hanging from the rafters of her own humble cottage. Not when a coil in her gut warned that she would be taken next.

Terrible dreams and pain strong enough to freeze her muscles always came as warning that Alpha arrival was imminent. A blessing and a curse she dared not share. A secret of such magnitude… an unexplainable alarm that cautioned of their arrival? Should the Alphas learn of it, and find the settlement empty? Everyone would be hunted and punished… and she would be executed for insubordination.

No matter what she had to endure, she would never leave her mother desolate and alone.

No matter the agony or sickness or fear that descended with their ships.

Season after season, Morgaine had bested it. She had carried her secret into the woods and would do so again.

Yet that morning, her body was a twisting ball of agony, and she was almost unable to move.

Groaning, Morgaine threw her legs over the side of the bed. Braced against the cot, it took four tries before she was able to lift her torso. The movement of pitching forward sent each limb into a spasm, leaving the girl falling into a haphazard pile on the ground.

Fresh rushes muffled the thump of her collapse, but Morgaine tossed a frightened glance to where her mother softly snored nearby. Her graceless landing hadn't disturbed the woman's sleep, but the rising pained scream trying to rip its way out of Morgaine's chest would.

Biting her tongue as the fresh wave of hellish fire churned her guts into knotted agony, Morgaine forced herself to be still and silent. Her mother slept on, rolling over to snore all the louder.

Blood-laced spittle dribbled from the corner of Morgaine's mouth when she parted her teeth and dared suck in a breath.

It was imperative not to wake her mother, but by

the spirits, she *had* to get out of their cottage before she gave herself away.

That way, the woman would not have to lie if questioned. That way, the responsibility would be squarely on Morgaine's shoulders if her noncompliance was ever uncovered.

As if she too understood that some things were better left unsaid, after all these years, her mother had never questioned why Morgaine was conveniently gone when Alphas stole through the settlement—had no inkling that pain warned her child of the invasion.

It was Morgaine's great shame to bear—for every time she fled, others were taken who might have found refuge if they'd only known to hide. But if she were to warn her neighbors, she would be exposed. Others would know there was something wrong with her, that she was a lawbreaker, and she knew in her heart that should an Alpha lay eyes on her...

...they would ruin her.

With her only aunt dead, her mother would be alone with no other family to comfort her.

If Morgaine were taken, who would know how to find toxic hicklim berries to make the lovely green-dyed fabric her mother was famed for sewing? Who would collect eggs and pluck the chickens? How would her mother survive alone?

Morgaine would chew her own arm off if it meant keeping the woman safe.

Boiling fever and excruciating pain? Morgaine deserved them for keeping her secrets. The good woman snoring in the corner did not.

A wave of nausea curled Morgaine's tongue into a bowl. Gagging, she convulsed, watched the room grow darker, and was moments away from losing consciousness right there on the floor.

The males had come closer. There was no time to waste.

Arms weightier than stone pushed a traitorous body to stand on shaky legs. Biting back another scream, she grabbed the first garment she could reach. Fingers twisted by cramps fumbled the laces of the gown, leaving it hanging indecently off her shoulders. There would be no boots. She could hardly lift a foot to move forward, stumbling one perilous step at a time until she reached the humble cottage's only door.

The latch was maneuvered, her quiet retreat unnoticed in the gloomy morning hours.

Clawing for the nearest handhold, she braced against a neighbor's dwelling to steady a body wracked with tremors and felt a trickle run down her thigh. She had wet herself.

And she couldn't care less.

Cold sweat and misty morning air did nothing to cool the fire crackling through flesh and bones.

Every cell in her body demanded that she just lay still and submit to her fate.

How many more seasons could she crawl without screaming before a neighbor found her sobbing in a ditch?

Already she'd chewed her tongue bloody, dug her fingernails into her palms until they bled. Anything it took to stay quiet.

The Alphas were close, the shooting stars in the sky a sign they descended through the atmosphere and would touch down in mere minutes. They'd be storming through the village before the sun rose, and should she be unable to move, they would find her while ransacking the settlement, convulsing beside a mud-splattered animal pen.

Pulling desperation around her like a comforting blanket, Morgaine forced her body forward another step.

It took her over an hour to stagger the short distance to the settlement's boundary, another hour to lurch down the road to the nearest tree line.

No matter the wildlife, the forests were safe enough if one knew where to tread—safer by far than the massive warriors, with their vermilion armor, their weapons, and their cruelty. While the Alphas went shelter to shelter taking what they desired, Morgaine would collapse beyond their notice.

While they pillaged, she'd suffer alone.

She'd suffer a thousand days of agony for her

mother. She'd suffer the guilt of watching other families grieve their stolen children upon her return.

And once the sun set, their ships bursting with stolen people and goods, the Alphas would have no reason to linger. They would leave. They always did. And her pain would end as it always did.

Morgaine only had to stay unseen for one day.

But freedom wouldn't count if she were found writhing on the road.

A sharp turn to the right, and the grass' morning damp began to weigh down her dragging skirts. Fabric caught on her ankles and sent Morgaine sprawling against a dogwood tree.

Ten paces from the stone path, she lay unable to move a single step further.

Under her body, the ground was mud, soggy with fresh water from the stream just out of reach. One sip, a mouthful of sweetness, she craved it more than life. But Morgaine could not move no matter how she strained.

Curled upon herself, the crackling agony traveled through bone and organs. Sobbing against the dirt, time lost all meaning—an eternity of fire in the center of the ugliest hell.

For hours she lay, fevered and ill, gnarled roots digging into her spine. Hours lost in pain.

And then the Alpha ships began to rise into the

setting sun. One by one, dozens of vessels filled the sky and began to disappear beyond the atmosphere.

With them went the source of her torment.

Expanding her ribs in her first full breath since before the sun had risen, Morgaine twitched her fingers, then her toes—arms, legs, all movement slowly beginning to return. Damp with sour sweat, caked in drying mud, she crawled wild, unkempt, and exhausted toward the nearest source of comfort.

Trickling water was gulped by the mouthful. Hands and face rinsed clean of muck and crusted tears. There was nothing that could be done for her dress. Grass has stained it, sodden mud having smeared her mother's fine embroidery.

Throat burning as if grated raw by sand, she told herself to get up.

Stomach sloshing, nauseated, Morgaine found her feet and let the tree at her back bear her weight until she might find the strength to walk home.

With a weak smile, she chanted a prayer for forgiveness.

The spirits did not listen.

2

"Where have you been, Morgaine?"

"What?" Unbound hair ratted from a day thrashing in the mud, Morgaine shoved it off her sweating forehead. She darted her eyes from the dusty path to find her neighbor frowning mightily. "I was…"

Clucking, Hanna's gaze lingered on the muddy dress hanging open at Morgaine's bosom. "Cover your shift, you tramp. You didn't even do up your laces after letting one of them tumble you in the grass. You're no different than your—"

The coming slander wasn't to be tolerated. Instant fury overshadowed any embarrassment, and Morgaine took a step toward the woman. "I would never let those pigs touch me!"

Hands to her hips, Hanna shook her head. "So you

say, shameless girl. How many did you spread for trying to buy leniency for your mother?"

Ice went down her back, and all affront dissolved into stomach-gnawing anxiety. "What about my mother?"

"Elizabeta dared lie when you could not be found."

"What lie? She didn't know where I was." Impatient for real answers, Morgaine made a grab for the plump goodwife's arm. "Did they hurt her?"

"You should have accepted my boy when he offered for you!" Glaring down at the bit of exposed breast, she snorted. "You brought their anger on yourself with your trickery and sluttish ways."

"What did they do to her?" The desperate question was shrieked loud enough to draw the eyes of those nearby. "Tell me now!"

It was easy for her neighbor to brush off Morgaine's weak grip. Easier still for the old dame to taunt, "The rules apply to you as they apply to us all, you horrid girl. Go see for yourself what has been done. My Cassius was lucky to be free of you."

Unsteady on her feet, Morgaine threw a frightened glace around for a hint.

The settlement was still in a state of uproar, baskets tossed about on the street after Alphas had laid claim to whatever valuable thing had been stored inside.

The muddy walks were littered with loose feathers, chickens and ducks having been snatched from their coops and carried off. Livestock ran wild after pens had been left open, the heartiest beasts gone to the Alphas' ships.

Weeping, there was so much weeping.

The baker's wife was beside herself, sobbing over one of her twins. It was obvious why: his mismatching towheaded brother was missing. Beside her, her husband's eye swelled shut as he stood there, dumbstruck.

Crops had been ripped from beds, bits of furnishings thrown about as if selected, then discarded when something better caught an Alpha's eye.

Two male bodies swung from the gallows in the square. Morgaine knew them both, one of the corpses dressed in red cloth she had woven herself.

Sick to her stomach at the sight, Morgaine stumbled forward and clawed her way through the building throng. There was little time to sort out who else was weeping for their loved ones, what had been taken, for even from a distance, Morgaine saw a crowd had formed outside her small home.

Neighbors stood in the dusty road, several trampling the garden beds, ruining heads of lettuce almost ready for consumption.

Something was very wrong.

Fist pressed to the stitch in her side, Morgaine

broke into a graceless run, rudely shoving those aside who stood in her way.

Over and over she heard settlers muttering her name with repugnance once they caught sight of her. It wasn't the gaping, muddy dress, or the fact her long golden hair was free of a covering.

In their eyes, for some unknown reason, she'd committed a great crime.

It didn't matter what they thought, or the slander they might toss at her back as she fought her way forward. The only thing that mattered was finding her mother.

With a great shove, she budged the last line of townsfolk apart and found... nothing.

Her cottage stood as it always did, the cheerfully painted wooden door shut.

Creeping closer, on the verge of being ill, Morgaine reached for the latch and froze.

A terrifying voice boomed behind it. *"Her scent is abundant in this shack, old woman. Slick and fear, I can taste them in the air! There will be no more patience for your lies. Tell me where she is, or you will be tied up in the center of town and burned to death for the trouble you've caused."*

Ear to the door, breath caught in her lungs, Morgaine heard the dulcet voice of her mother's steady, submissive reply. *"I assure you again, none reside here but I, sir. I am a tailor and live a modest life. Customers come to me, to this room, to be fitted for their clothing. It must be one of them you smell."*

A dangerous growl shook the walls. *"Your neighbors tell a different tale, madam. You have a daughter. Her name is Morgaine... and you have allowed her to age out of our sight to the point that she is now full-grown. The child is not your property. She belongs to the Alphas, and you shall give her up."*

"My only child died years ago. Whoever told you differently is mistaken. Take any of my goods you desire. See, prized cloth, woven and dyed to a deep red? It's yours. How about embroidered tatted lace for your wife? Look here, this is my finest work. Beyond these wares, I have nothing else to offer you, great Alpha."

Each hair on the back of Morgaine's neck stood at attention, her heart in her throat upon hearing the Alpha cruelly bark, *"Have her bound in the square. If she will not answer with honesty, she will be made an example of and left there to rot."*

"No!" Hand to the latch, Morgaine thrust the door inward, desperate to save her mother. "Don't hurt her! I am here."

In the cottage's dim light, two huge, unwanted males dominated the small chaotic space. Amongst tossed furniture and shattered possessions they stood: pristine armor, weapons hanging at their waists and slung across their backs.

Both poured every ounce of their attention over her, each male unnaturally still and unblinking.

The door shut with a bang at her back.

Eyes welling, Morgaine stumbled forward and repeated. "I'm here."

The nearest soldier took a step toward her. In response, she drew in a breath, ready to beg for her mother's life. One deep inhalation, and Morgaine became stone.

It was as if she could taste the intruders in the back of her throat. Embers... it was like breathing in scorching fire that burned from the inside out.

She couldn't speak to beg for amnesty. She couldn't fall to her knees.

She couldn't breathe.

Blinking madly, a wheeze caught in her chest.

Wide-eyed, she cut a panicked glance to her mother. An Alpha's hand was wrapped around the woman's throat, her taut body jammed against the wall. Gone was the calm-voiced merchant. Shaking from terror, she reached for her child.

Desperate to cling to her mother, unable to move, Morgaine felt warm tears slip from her eyes. She tried, she tried with everything in her being to reach back.

Instead, the floor met her knees when a viscous cramp tore up her calves and left her sprawling. The genuflection was not an act of supplication. Not when her hands had clawed into the floor as if it might save her.

Lack of air left her giddy, weak, and on the verge of unconsciousness.

Through the tangle of her hair, she saw the closest soldier's boots approach.

Amusement colored his gibe. "Your nonexistent daughter has returned."

Fingers splayed, Morgaine stared at the rushes under her palms, babbling out anything she thought might appease the men who tormented her mother. "I was in the woods... gathering berries."

An unwelcome finger hooked her chin, forcing her to raise her face for inspection. The man touching her, the intruder who had wrecked her home, was larger than any male in her village. Huge. Mean. A weather-beaten face frowned down at her. "And where are these berries?"

"I couldn't..." she could not have gathered berries earlier, just as in that moment she could not form proper words. Silent tears dripped down dirty cheeks. "I love my mother."

"Hush, girl." The stranger held her eyes, cupped her face in his rough palms, and offered a soft smile.

It did not lessen the hardness of him, not in the slightest.

On the verge of bawling, Morgaine begged, "Please…"

At her entreaty, the stranger began to produce the most beautiful music.

Never had air rumbled with such perfect warmth. From under the vivid armor across his chest, deep reverberations made the world new. The resonating noise held the power to loosen her locked muscles—Morgaine suddenly able to suck in greedy gulps of air.

Baffled, she gaped. The Alpha purred in the way the courting men of her settlement purred—the way her fat neighbor's son, Cassius, had purred when he'd offered her flowers... but deeper... the sound so profound her body felt as if it were weightless in a vast body of water.

"Keep your eyes open, renegade." Inundated with rich vibration, a voice rough around the edges grew remarkably smooth. As did his touch when his thumb wiped her cheeks clean of tears. "I wish to hear your name from your own lips."

Anything, she would do anything to see her mother set free. Even the unspeakable thing her neighbor Hanna had accused her of moments before. Thick-tongued, she whispered, "Morgaine."

The Alpha's attention may have been centered on her, the soldier turning her chin left to right as he looked her over, but his words were for her mother. "You are very lucky, old woman, that this one is exceptionally beautiful."

Desperate to reach her child, her mother fought the

second soldier who still held her by the throat. "Leave her be. You can't have her!"

The wild effort produced no change in the situation. The male batted her mother's hands away as if swatting a fly and spoke to his comrade. "The girl is many years past the age she should have been collected. The Omega is most likely damaged."

"No." The back of the purring Alpha's fingers tripped down Morgaine's neck, tracing the line of flesh exposed above the open bodice of her filthy dress. He pulled her shift aside until the pink tip of her nipple came into his sight. And then he touched her there, circling secret flesh with the pad of his finger. "This one is perfect."

Toes curling, a strange croak caught in Morgaine's throat. She lost sight of her mother's struggles in the corner. She forgot that she should have been pleading for mercy. She forgot her name.

When the Alpha groaned in approval and palmed the full weight of her breast, Morgaine felt the world slip away. "I... I'm dying."

Those sad words moved her purring tormentor to reach out and catch her listing body before it hit the ground. In one sweep he hoisted her to his chest and purred all the louder. Voice unbelievably gentle, the stranger put his lips to her ear. "Come, Omega, I know what will make you feel better."

3

A lovely sensation of floating in cream… of safety and warmth, enveloped her body. Morgaine was wrapped in velvet reassurance—the impression so rich, so perfectly contenting, that when lashes fluttered open, she was certain she had passed into the spirit world.

Or so she thought. Lingering soreness in her shoulder began to throb with the smallest movement. Next came awareness of the dry sting of abraded palms. And her knees, her knees were stiff with scabs, joints and muscles aching.

The dead were not supposed to know pain.

A soft whimper escaped parted lips.

Blinking twice, she found her eyes were unable to see even a hand before her face.

She had gone to the dark place of suffering instead.

Fear chased away the last remnants of her false sense of security.

Engulfed in stygian darkness, cocooned in something softer than rabbit fur, Morgaine began to hyperventilate. It was more than her inability to see, it was the scent: spice, musk, salt, sweat... all decidedly male and not a single one familiar.

Alphas.

She was surrounded, locked in pitch black, and she had no idea which way to run.

The room seemed to answer the growing thump of her heart, and soft light emanated from an unknown source.

The glow grew, and the wide-eyed girl found that though the scent of many males filled the room, she was, in fact, alone.

Alone and sprawled within a cushioned pit.

Covering her body were fragments of white fur, scattered like fallen flower petals over her while she'd slept. From each pelt emanated the aroma of a different Alpha. A hundred of them, maybe more.

The fragrance was disturbingly pleasant, as was the fur's texture, but the uncertainty of why such a thing had been done encouraged only a raw feeling of disgust. Worse still, under the soft pile, her dress and undergarments had been removed. Those scented scraps were the only thing covering her nakedness.

Should she stand, not a single piece would be large enough to cover more than one breast at a time.

That frightened her the most. Whoever put her in that cushioned hollow wanted her naked, with no recourse to indulge her modesty once she woke.

They had left her utterly vulnerable.

Edging back until her shoulders met the curved side of the sleeping pit, Morgaine cast off the reeking furs, pulling long, golden curls over her shoulders like a cloak. Drawing skinned knees under her chin, she found someone had washed the mud from her hands, arms, feet, but under her nails, traces of grit remained.

Cringing, Morgaine knew who that someone had to be. The same man who had unabashedly pulled open her dress and let his fingers twist the tip of her breast. The horrid Alpha had touched her in a way only husbands were allowed to touch... and he had done all of this right in front of her mother.

Who cared if he'd also tended to the many bruises on her body? It didn't matter that they had been smeared with dried healing unguent, that they no longer hurt when poked.

Staring at the flaking orange signs of his attention, she felt great shame prickle all over her skin.

I know what will make you feel better. That's what he'd said.

She wanted to rub his touch off her skin, grabbing at a random fur scrap to scour the medicine away. Underneath, the bruises had already begun to fade to yellow. Soon they would be completely gone. But the memory of his fingers toying with her breast… that would never leave her mind.

The scabs at her knees looked almost healed. They would shed, the skin would be new, and all the wounds she'd earned trying to be free of Alpha monsters would be gone.

Just as her dress was gone. Just as her mother was gone.

Mother…

Morgaine could still hear her mother screaming, begging, as the Alpha scooped her up against his rough armor and carted her out the door. And what had she done? Nothing, she'd hung from his arms like a stuffed doll, eyes rolling back—her last view the cottage rafters hung with their bunches of drying herbs.

There had never even been a goodbye.

Because Morgaine had fallen asleep cradled by a monster who'd threatened to burn her mother alive.

In that moment, she couldn't hate herself more.

Choking cries, hot tears, were lost against her knees. Her skin might be healing, the bone deep ache in her muscles slowly abating, but the pain in her heart was forever.

Morgaine hoped they came soon to kill her. She prayed that however the Alphas saw fit to execute her would be horrific. She deserved to suffer.

Just as she knew her mother was suffering now.

"It is not necessary to mourn. You're in no danger, Omega."

Where he'd come from she did not know. It didn't matter. All that mattered was that a stranger was standing over where she'd curled up in despair.

With a startled shriek, Morgaine flew from the cushions. Throwing a knee over the ledge of the sunken bed, she scrambled out and ran naked to the farthest corner of the room.

One look at that Alpha and all her hubris in wishing for death vanished. It was too hard to face the end bravely when the executioner was actually there to drag her to it.

Cowering behind her hair, visibly shaking, she sobbed, "Don't touch me!"

Stoic in his regard, the Alpha had not moved, and the ease of his stance gave no indication he was preparing to chase her. The stranger in vermilion armor was stone. "My name is Sergeant Uriel. As a mated Alpha of proper rank, I have been tasked with managing your transition."

Desperate to put something between her naked body and his armored one, Morgaine abandoned her corner and ran behind a table laden with food. Lifting a chair before her, she clutched it close to her chest, ready to swing it as a potential weapon if he thought to pursue.

Adrenaline spiked her heart rate, made her pupils contract, and even added spite to her tongue. "What happened to my mother?"

"You were procured by Corporal Esin. Any penalties that were inflicted on the Beta woman you will need to ask him about yourself." Sergeant Uriel took a step closer. "Put the chair down."

Modesty be damned. She raised her weapon higher. "No."

"You were ill when he found you, and would not have survived much longer without the care of a vigilant Alpha." Another measured step brought Sergeant Uriel closer. "Omegas require specific attention. Here, you will receive that attention."

That word again, that hated title used to make naughty children behave else they be taken. To be Omega was to be something terrible. "I am not an Omega. Omegas are dangerous, and I've never hurt a soul. I've never even broken a law."

The man stopped his advance, cocking a brow as if to point out the falsehood of her last statement.

She didn't know where the boldness came from. Perhaps it was because she knew her end was near. What point was there in holding her tongue now? "There is no law that says colonists have to be present when Alphas invade to steal our crops and livestock."

"Impudence is not tolerated, Omega. Neither are lies. I'll forgo teaching you a lesson this once, as you are adapting to this *new situation* and are visibly upset. Yet I caution you not to test my benevolence."

The way he'd spoken the word *lesson,* how his voice had dropped and grown cold, put ice in Morgaine's veins. Her skin grew clammy, the hairs on her arms stood up on end. Even her throat grew tight. More tears came, and with much less confidence, she said, "I'm not an Omega."

A decisive step her way, face one of severe disapproval, and the Alpha murmured, "You have no concept of what would have happened to you if left in Beta society. Had you, you would have submitted to the first Alpha to cross your path and begged him to take you away."

Never. Never in a million years would she have done such a thing. Such thoughts didn't need to be spoken aloud. Morgaine's disgust was written all over her face.

Sergeant Uriel was not waylaid by her narrowed eyes or sneer. He pressed forward another step. "At your first estrous, you would have been raped by every capable male in your village, the population of your settlement fighting one another to mount you until you died. The violence would not have been their fault. It would have been yours for presuming to hide from our eyes." Another measured step. "Omegas are indeed very dangerous."

She did not understand the term *estrous*, but the picture he painted was nausea inducing. "You're sick."

He never wavered, Uriel's expression neutral as he said, "Not one of them—pubescent boys, grown men, the elderly—would have been able to stop themselves. How many would have died for your pride? Your mother surely would have been murdered had she tried to keep you from the rabid crowd."

Mouth sour, breath shallow and irregular, Morgaine shook her head. "My neighbors are peaceful people. I don't know what your *estrous* is, but things like you describe do not happen in my settlement."

The Alpha gestured to her right. "Recordings of such moments have been set aside for your required viewing so that you may understand what would have been your fate."

Like magic, the wall came alive with images. Air filling with screams, moans, all nature of horrific noises, Morgaine looked without thinking and saw horrors. Bodies climbing over bloody bodies, a throng of violence moving like a twisting mass of snakes. In the center of it was a slack-mouthed girl, her eyes pitch black as she was mauled beyond recognition.

Morgaine could not tell if the female was fighting

the mob or pulling them nearer. All she saw were the fluids and the gore.

Never had she seen a naked male's erect member. A great many were displayed on that living wall… grotesque and bulbous and bloody. Never again did she want to see another.

Yet it was impossible to tear her eyes away.

The screams grew louder.

Dropping the chair to press her hands to her ears did not block out horrific screeches that would haunt her until she died.

Just like the girl on the screen died.

Yet, the poor Omega's death had not stopped the mob from fighting for any of the girl's orifices they might penetrate.

Her corpse was literally torn apart.

Morgaine bent forward, dry heaving over her feet, and Sergeant Uriel closed the final distance between them. Her long golden hair was gathered away from an ashen face so the screen was still in her view. Fist tight against her roots, Sergeant Uriel pulled, forcing her head to angle back so she might watch the scene in its entirety.

The story on the wall continued, the man at her side narrating what was projected before her. "When their rut subsided, the men were beside themselves with shame. The entire settlement had to be eradicated and replaced. Every last settler died because Esmeralda, like you, had *avoided* collection."

The next images were of the bodies laid out side by side in a mass grave. All ages, all stations, everyone just as the Alpha had claimed.

Despite his grip on her hair, Morgaine fell to her knees.

"Shall we view Chen's death next?"

Wailing, "No," Morgaine conceded, willing to say anything to make it stop. "I am whatever you say I am."

Sergeant Uriel's touch grew gentle. Leaning down, he put an arm around her middle and helped the distraught girl to her feet. A deep purr colored his next words. "We have learned it is best to be direct when faced with the rare feral. You must be made to recognize that what was done was done for your benefit. Here, Omegas are loved, protected by Alphas. Understanding this is key—"

Bile rose up to burn the back of her throat. "Loved?"

The sergeant sat her in the very chair she'd thought to wield as a weapon, assuring with a rich purr and careful touch. "Yes, *loved*. I love my mate very much."

There had been no love in any Alpha action Morgaine had ever seen. Even this one had already threatened her, yanked at her hair, and made demands. That's all Alphas did: take and harm.

They didn't know how to love.

But they knew how to strip a sleeping girl naked, terrorize, and show her things that would give her nightmares for years. Revolted, Morgaine choked out, "Did you force the woman you love to watch that?"

Sergeant Uriel reached for a pitcher, poured a glass of water, and pressed it to Morgaine's lips. "It was not a lesson she required."

Teeth chattering, cold and unable to stop shaking, Morgaine refused to swallow the offered water. He tipped the glass. When she began to sputter and water ran down her chin, he gripped her hair in his fist again.

He didn't pull; he just made it clear he would correct her if he had to. "You will drink this water."

Their eyes met, inflexible yet equally forgiving, and Morgaine knew she'd lost whatever battle had just taken place.

She would lose all battles. He wanted her to know that.

He wanted submission.

And it felt like that was worse than death.

Again, she started to cry.

The Alpha's purr increased significantly. His point had been made, and the slump of her shoulders was concession enough. He refilled the glass and lifted it to her lips a second time.

She didn't fight him, let herself be lulled by the purr enough to manage the rapid gulps required before he might tip the glass back further and drown her in it. Once drained, he pulled it away, and set it on the table.

Sucking in air, Morgaine stared. Sergeant Uriel was old enough to be her father. Gray marked the brown hair at his temples, there were creases on his face, and the hands that had touched her were callused from years of use. This was a man hard through and through.

And yet he purred.

Morgaine wilted under his unflinching gaze. Hopeless, exhausted, and scared, she whispered, "I want to go home."

He ran a pat over her tangled hair and held back any cruelty as he asked, "After what you just saw, knowing that would be your fate?"

Her eyes closed and she shuddered, shrinking further into herself. Of course she didn't want that. Even now she saw the mass grave and it was as if the faces in it were people she knew, grew up with, loved.

Pathetic, Morgaine could not help but call for the one thing that might make it all go away. "I want my mother."

The weight of his hand left her hair, just as the

gentleness left his voice. Gruff he said, "Soon you will have a mate. A night with him and your mother will be forgotten." The Alpha straightened, pointing at the table before her. "Now you will eat. When you have finished, bathe yourself in that corner over there. If these two things have not taken place by the time I have returned, there will be another *lesson*."

4

———

The bizarre toilet, the deep, gilded tub—both items of such a personal nature were exposed to the room.

No screen, no curtain… they were just there out in the open.

Sergeant Uriel had warned her, presented two clear commands, and then he had taken his purr and his presence away. Curled in on herself, she had not even seen where he'd gone.

Having slid from the chair the moment the weight of his hand had left her back, she'd crouched down on the floor, trying to make herself as small as possible.

Lessons.

Her mind would break if another lesson had to be endured.

That poor Omega. From what Morgaine had seen, the girl had done no evil. *Evil had been done to her.*

Why? Why would her townsfolk commit such a heinous act?

The questions came out unbidden, muttered brokenly to the air the same way Morgaine had prayed to the spirits. And just like when she prayed to the spirits, no answer came.

The only response she received was the room growing colder.

Skin prickling no matter how she ran her hands up and down her arms, she began to shiver, and would have given anything for a blanket.

Naked, utterly exposed to an empty room, feeling the cold seep into her bones… was messing with her head.

She let out a frustrated breath and saw fog hang in the air before her eyes. Seeing the mist dissipate, knowing the room had been made cold on purpose, pushed her over the edge.

"Help!" There was no door in the room to bang upon, the frantic Omega scrambling off the floor in search of a way out. All the walls were smooth, unchanging, and icy to the touch. "Please, anyone. HELP ME! I need to get back to my mother!"

She banged on the reflective surface, she begged.

Silence.

Growing colder by the second, her teeth began to

chatter. Arms tight around her middle, she understood there were only two options: the odd sunken bed full of smelly bits of fur, or the exposed tub that had miraculously begun filling itself.

Twirling steam rose from the surface, beckoning her to step into the heated water and find comfort.

Eat, the Alpha had ordered. Then bathe, he had said.

Do these things or suffer another *lesson*.

Crying in earnest, her attention went to the table.

Legs heavy enough to be weighted with sand, carried her to it. Her naked rear set upon an embroidered cushion. It was a pretty chair, one that could have been stolen from one of the finer houses in her settlement. Morgaine would have preferred the polished wooden seats that her mother had provided in their simple cottage—just as she would have preferred the smell of fresh baked bread to the rich dishes lain out before her.

The tears had dried up as she looked over the spread, or maybe they had frozen on her cheeks. Even the panic seemed to have grown ice cold.

Numb, inside and out, she made herself reach out for the nearest piece of food. A bite of sweet sliced fruit hit her tongue, but all she could think of was blood and parts of a man that had drawn that blood.

Ugly parts.

Parts that she'd witnessed just moments ago spurting grotesque fluid on the face of that dead girl.

Morgaine threw up every bite.

Less concerned about her body's rejection of the food, and more concerned about looming punishment, she forced her head up and looked around like a spooked animal for the predator she knew was hiding in the shadows.

Except this room had no shadows. That odd glowing light came from everywhere and illuminated everything.

Certain she would be punished for the mess she'd made, Morgaine gave up. It was as if something else controlled her limbs, some sort of self-preservation forcing her to act. She stood, took a beleaguered step forward, and then another one.

The toilet was there.

First she vomited into it. Then, glassy eyed, she'd sat on the rim and tried to pee.

She couldn't squeeze out a drop.

The lights dimmed.

Urine splattered inside the bowl, as if a silent voice had commanded and her body had obeyed.

She staggered from her throne to the steaming tub.

Like the cushion and fur-filled sleeping pit, the tub was sunken into the ground and ornately decorated. An array of blue tiles, the patterns of flowers vining through the mosaic, warm soothing water...

Morgaine knew it was a lie.

Not one thing in this room had offered comfort in any measure: not the bed, not the food, not the strange toilet or this steaming pool.

The water began to swirl and offer up frothy bubbles.

Too cold to be properly startled, her only reaction was the insignificant widening of her eyes.

Rooms were supposed to have doors.

Tubs should not fill themselves.

Walls should not show horrors.

Was this hell?

Is this what she'd brought upon herself for lying to the village?

As if the room could read her thoughts, the very wall that had terrified her only moments before transformed in a rippling blur. In place of rape and murder, Morgaine was given a window. From corner to corner, the space displayed verdant forest. Even the air grew warmed by a soft wind and the chirp of birds.

Technology of this sort this did not exist in her settlement.

Wise enough to know there were no birds singing, no tree branches bending to soft breezes, she frowned at the view. It was nothing compared to forests, to *real* trees. The image, in its entirety, was an insult.

Gorge yourself on food most likely stolen from your settlement. Bathe, hair uncovered, like a whore.

Or watch more horrors…

There was no question.

Lowering her body into the steaming water, Morgaine kept her eye on that false view of the forest. She sank like a stone until the water hit her chin.

The heat stung limbs that had grown ice cold. It hurt.

She *wanted* it to hurt.

The tub whirled, streams of steam mixing with soap until more bubbles covered the surface.

The scent was not to her taste. The instant she wrinkled her nose, she would have sworn it altered. What had been roses became herbal... tolerable.

Nausea slowly subsided. Extreme exhaustion took its place.

Drawing a deep breath, she let her head slip beneath the water, listening to the churn and slosh until her lungs began to burn. She wanted to stay like that, in her own underwater world until her heart stopped.

But the tub began to drain on its own.

Her momentary sanctuary was stolen away.

Dripping wet, she sat in the empty bath and hung her head in her hands.

She recognized that the tub wasn't for comfort. It might be pretty, it might have smelled pleasant, but its purpose was for her to listen and obey.

To be clean because Sergeant Uriel had ordered it.

To be trapped within flower mosaic tiles because there was no towel and nowhere to hide.

She had not been able to get out, but *he* had found a way in. She'd heard the bootsteps, could smell who'd come to invade and stand in triumph over her.

Morgaine did not give him the honor of lifting her head or even addressing his presence.

The intruder began to purr.

Still, she refused to raise her neck and meet his eye. What was the point? "Is this what you had in mind when you claimed you knew what would make me *feel better*? Leaving me naked, wet, shamed, and frightened? Whatever punishment your people have decided I have coming, just get it over with."

An unwelcome hand came to rest on the top of her head. Voice just as gruff as she remembered from her cottage, said, "That is not an appropriate way to address an Alpha."

Disgusted that he would touch her, Morgaine squeezed her eyes shut. "Uriel? Was that his name, the one managing my *transition*?"

He corrected, "Sergeant Uriel."

Digging the heels of her palms against her lids, she pressed until she saw stars, and said, "*Sergeant Uriel* said only you could tell me what became of my mother."

"Look at me."

It was a gentle command, one Morgaine supposed

was intended to entice. But that was not why she raised her head. She did it because her heart was breaking, and she needed to know her mother lived.

The man who had fondled her breasts in her home, who had threatened the person she loved most, who had dragged her away as if he had the right, smiled.

Unlike Sergeant Uriel, he no longer wore the vermilion armor. He was dressed in knit fabric that stretched across his chest yet left his arms bare. Loose pants hung from his waist, held up with what looked to be no more than a drawstring. Casual.

At her attention, the soldier tried to soften the harshness of his craggy voice with gentle speech. "My name is Corporal Esin."

There was only one name that mattered in this moment. "My mother's name is Elizabeta. Your friend held her by the neck when you threatened to burn her alive. And then... I couldn't see what was done to her."

He stroked her head, seemingly distracted by the way her curls hung limp while weighted with water.

Wary, angry, scared, Morgaine whispered, "Please tell me she's okay."

Brown eyes met hers. Clear and concise he answered, "Her face was branded for treason."

It was like a knife in the heart. Throwing off the hand that played with her hair, daring to raise an expression full of hate toward the very soldier who had stolen her from her house, Morgaine spat on the man kneeling at the edge of the tub.

Indifferent, Corporal Esin wiped her spittle from his cheek. "It was the most lenient punishment I could offer. Considering the offense, she should have been executed… not paid as handsomely as she was for the trouble. Be glad she still lives and has a fortune to see to her comfort."

Blood boiling, Morgaine drew up and hissed, "If I ever find a way to brand your face in exchange for what you've done, I will do it. Better yet, I'd rather see you dead."

Her threat made his smile fade, and the Alpha's expression grew dark. "If you continue to speak this way, I will be forced to act, and you will not like the outcome."

Morgaine was so very tempted to scream at him, to strike him, but her tongue grew fat and all that came were silent, angry tears.

Rising from his crouch, he offered her a hand. "Step from the tub."

Not only did she balk at the thought of touching him, the thought of him seeing her bared breasts and mound was more than she could handle. She shook her head and shrank further away.

"It was not a request, Morgaine. Get up so that you might be dried."

She swallowed, eyes showing every ounce of her

trepidation and humiliation. "It is not right for you to ask such a thing or look at me this way."

"Because you are naked?"

Nodding, she added the other cause for concern. "And you are purring. It's only done when a male is... interested. I don't want to—"

He finished the sentence for her. "You don't want to be mounted."

Before this horrid day, she'd never heard sex described that way. *Mounted*, climbed over, held down —her mind filling with images of what happened to the Omega on the wall... the writhing bodies... the screams.

If he tried to do such a thing, she would die.

He extended his hand even further. "I have not been given clearance to penetrate you today."

If Corporal Esin thought to offer reassurance, he'd failed. Morgaine did not know what was hidden in his statement, but it certainly was not a comforting thing to hear. "Today?"

"There is much that must be explained, and I refuse to have this conversation while you are dripping wet and shivering. Come out of the tub or I will climb in and get you."

What dignity was there in being dragged out like a child? None. There was none.

Breaking her eyes from his, she turned her face to the wall, covered her breasts with her arm, her mound with her free hand, and tried not to cringe when he put his hands on her body to help her manage the steps.

After pulling her to stand atop an absorbent mat, he produced fabric softer than the finest weave her mother had ever produced. Starting with her cheeks, blotting the tears, Esin wielded his huge hands deftly and with caution... until he reached her breasts.

She refused to budge her arm.

So much stronger than her, he took a solid grip of her wrist, and forced her shield from her chest.

Every muscle in her body went stiff. The arm he held shook, her breath grew shallow, and she was moments away from screaming for help.

Purring all the louder, his eyes tracked over the swell of a generous bosom. "You are a pretty one, renegade."

Towel forgotten, he measured the weight of her right breast. His fingers pawed and explored, a determined thumb swirling her nipple.

Seeing that pink flesh grow tight, his breath caught, voice husky from excitement. "Tell me, has another male touched you this way?"

There had been caresses from boys in the village, a few stolen kisses, but none would have dared to grab her breasts. The fact a stranger was doing it now, that he still held her captive by one arm, was mortifying. "You mean without permission?"

The corner of his lip ticked upward. He was not at

all ashamed. "Upon your initial examination your hymen was found partly ruptured before it was removed for your future comfort—"

She abandoned boring a hole in the wall with her eyes, slack-jawed. "What?"

"Here." He moved the towel to her mound, tapping where she pressed her legs together as if to block his view. "Your hymen."

She knew what a hymen was, and could not believe that some stranger had examined her close enough between her legs to see it.

Face turning red with a blend of fury and embarrassment, trying to think up something worthy to shriek, Morgaine was silenced by the Alpha's next probe. "Have you touched yourself there? Slipped your fingers into your body? Did you use a tool to stimulate yourself? Or was it a Beta's attentions that damaged the membrane?"

"That is none of your business!"

"Actually, it is very much my business."

This was not to be borne. Degraded, Morgaine sneered and tried her damnedest to appear as undesirable as possible. "I have lain with many of the boys in my village."

Her answer amused him, Esin grinning. "Boys? Not men?"

"Uhh." Awkward in her reply, Morgaine fumbled. "I meant men. Lots of men."

"And you are lying." Chuckling, he ogled her body, tracing the embarrassed flush on her breasts. "You have never been with a boy *or a man*... let alone many of them. It was your own fingers that did the damage. Either that, or your age thinned it in preparation of your first estrous."

Of course she had explored that part of her body in the dark, but only a few times when her mother was out of their small one-roomed dwelling. And this brute had the gall to laugh at her? "How would you feel if I asked you intimate questions about your body?"

Eyes instantly smoldering, Esin licked his lips. "You can ask me anything. Anything you want." He drew closer, the towel falling from his hands so he might grip the nip of her waist. "Ask to see my body. Ask to touch me."

He pulled her flush and began to rub his body over chill-prickled flesh. Hard muscle and foreign fabric... the smell of a male, Morgaine could not push it off, evade, or even find the words to complain.

"Right now I am hard and eager to be inside you." He groaned at her ear. "I know you can smell it. You've been sniffing the air since I walked into the room. Just as I can smell you. My arousal makes you nervous, virgin renegade."

Hearing him speak so, hands to his stomach in an attempt to push away, she couldn't help but see that between his hips, fabric tented with a clear outline of an erection far bigger than any she'd seen in Esmeralda's mauling.

"There is only one way to overcome fear." Voice low and promising, he swore, "The instant I am granted permission to fuck you, I swear I will knot you so hard you'll adore only me. I will pump my seed into your belly while you come. *I* will be the one to show you what it is to be mated by an Alpha."

Intensely uncomfortable, unsure what he was speaking of, but very sure its nature was unwelcome, Morgaine began to struggle all the harder.

A rough growl shot from his lips.

The resulting twinge between her legs, and Morgaine froze in abject horror. A tiny stream began to leak from her body, slowly making its way down her thigh.

Nostrils flaring, he sucked in a breath, dragging her closer by her imprisoned wrist. Settling a heavy arm around her back, Esin held her pinned, and panted, "I'm allowed to touch you."

Groaning with the effort, Morgaine tried and failed to shift him. "Please… let go."

The way his eyes ate her up, victorious and greedy, was nothing to his ravenous words. "Spread your legs for me and I will lick your sweet little cunt. Give me a taste and I'll let you come."

Morgaine shrieked when his fingers began to travel downward. "Stop!"

"Then you will touch me." Too rough, he forced her flared fingers down his torso until that hard, prodding growth he'd been smashing against her belly was flush to her palm. He closed her fingers around his erection and forced them up and down. On it went, the man making filthy groans, using her hand for his pleasure. "You feel that hard Alpha cock? You want to feel it throbbing inside you?"

Even with the fabric between them, Morgaine could feel the shape of his organ and thought she might retch. "I don't want to. Let go of me, you savage."

"Yes, you do. I can smell it." The man ignored her complaints, her flailing, and the tears, answering instead with a roar. Rocking his hips into her hand, the fabric under her palm grew wet. The male drew his lips back from his teeth, hissing.

He brought those teeth to her shoulder, growled like a feral wolf, and was just about to bite the terrified woman before a voice boomed from across the room. "That is enough, Corporal Esin. Step away from the Omega. Now."

Her assailant froze, not in fear, but in anger. Morgaine could see it in Esin's eyes, the thoughts of outright challenge, the temptation to violence at the intrusion.

More hot fluid splashed against her hand, having soaked through to drip and squish between her fingers.

Sergeant Uriel barked a reminder when it seemed Esin refused to obey. "Your claim would be forfeit should you break code. Collect yourself and heed orders."

Esin took a deep, unsteady breath. Looking down between their bodies, he luxuriated in the sight of her trapped hand on his dick and let out a groan. "May I rub it into her skin?"

What? Morgaine shook her head no, but the question had not been for her.

"You may not."

Capitulating, Esin gave Morgaine a lusty onceover before daring to press a kiss to her forehead. "Next time I will get my taste." He released her wrist, stepped back, and reluctantly obeyed his superior. "My apologies, Sergeant. She just smells so good."

With one last, expectant smile, Esin picked up the discarded towel and walked away.

5

———

When the wall opened, Esin retreated, and then the blasted thing grew whole as if no passage had ever existed. The smooth surface was back... smooth as glass. In fact, Morgaine could see her stricken, bared reflection in it —damp hair stuck to her skin, breasts flushed, eyes wild.

She looked at that reflection as if it were another person, muttering, "He took the towel with him." In shock, she shook the warm, dripping fluid from her hand. "I don't have a towel."

"I have brought you clothing." Sergeant Uriel slipped the lightest hint of fatherly cajoling into his command, gesturing to a place on the floor where he expected her to stand. "Come."

Breaking her attention away from the wall, feeling

utterly betrayed, Morgaine felt her lip quiver. "What just happened?"

A blunt answer was offered. "You brought him to release."

She had not brought him to anything. Esin had only taken. And now she reeked of that stuff that had oozed from the fabric over his… she didn't even want to find a word for that thing.

What would he have done to her had Sergeant Uriel not intervened? Distressed, she met the eyes of the older man. "Esin said he was not allowed to penetrate me *today*. Are you the one who decides when he rapes me?"

The sergeant began to purr. "It won't be rape."

At the magic of the vibration, air left her lungs on a painful exhale. A feeling of emptiness grew behind her breastbone. "I should just get it over with then. All of this, I want it to be over." Tears fell in earnest, her voice shaking worse than her slimy, soaked fingers. "Call him back in and let him finish. I will keep my eyes closed. Afterward, kill me."

Sergeant Uriel did not press her to approach again. Instead he crossed the room to her.

"No one is going to kill you. As I told you before, you're safe here."

"Safe?" That word must have meant something very different in this place. "He just…" her voice failed "…on my hand."

"Omega, the Alpha did not hurt you. His behavior was perfectly acceptable in reaction to your sexual excitement."

Gaping, all she could manage was a stuttered, "I told him to stop."

"Your genitals responded. The scent of slick is unmistakable. Your mind must be trained to acknowledge what your body already knows."

Arms around her middle, shaking like a leaf, Morgaine barely managed a sneer. "And what does my body know?"

"That you exist to submit. That there will be joy and pleasure in obedience. That Alphas are the only males capable of bringing you proper release."

What would her mother think if she had seen this? The sweet woman would have been appalled. Females in the settlement would never have been put upon in this way.

Ashamed down to her core, Morgaine looked back at her fluid-smeared hand, "I need to wash this off."

"That is unnecessary, offensive even to the Alpha who gave you his scent. Now, hold still while I dress you." Draped over Sergeant Uriel's arm was a cloth of royal blue, the same shade as her eyes. He lifted it over her head, arranging the long panel to hang from her neck. The garment left her back bared, the two hanging ends doing little more than swathing each breast. Around her waist he fashioned the two tails, knotting them, twisting, and fussing until one panel fell in front to cover her sex, the other kissed the skin over her rear.

There was no modesty in such clothing. Every curve, every hint of secret flesh was on display if she so much as breathed.

"All Omegas of breeding age wear such a garment. Your mate's rank and title will be embroidered on the back panel." Next, he pointed to the fabric over her mound. "And here. Should another Alpha see you, they will know to whom you belong.

"The panels across your chest can be pulled aside to bare your breasts for your mate. Eventually, they will facilitate the easy feeding of an infant. Below the waist nothing constrictive will impede mutual pleasure. Should you grow aroused, your slick will saturate your thighs, not the fabric. And it is easy to remove for mating."

Slick... there was that word again.

"Slick?"

As if to demonstrate the garment's easy access, Sergeant Uriel reached under the front panel and abruptly swiped through the remnants of leaking fluid smeared between her thighs. He even went so far as to hold his fingers before her eyes so she might see how the pads of his fingers slipped when rubbed together. "Slick. I assume you grasp its purpose?"

Uncertain if it was possible to be more mortified, heat rushed to Morgaine's face.

The cretin had the gall to look marginally amused. "Omegas respond to Alpha overtures by preparing their bodies for vigorous mating. Slick is released. Alphas, in turn, grow excited. Your pheromones demand that they fill you with seed. The corporal gave you seed. Instead of shaking off his offering, you should have rubbed it between your legs or across your breasts. Next time, do not repeat the same mistaken behavior."

All of this insanity was too much. She fell to her knees, gripping at his legs, and begged for mercy. "If I could have a real dress, a modest dress, he wouldn't see the slick. He wouldn't want to touch—"

Ignoring her protest, Uriel yanked at her arm until Morgaine wobbled to her feet. In response to her theatrics, he gave a tug to the fabric at her waist. One undone knot, and the garment began to fall to the floor. "This is a real dress, but if you don't want it..."

Snatching the slipping edges before her nipples were on display, Morgaine clutched it to her chest, and backed away as if he were more of a threat than Esin. "I want it."

Their eyes met, Uriel ceasing his purr as if to drive home what was at stake should she be difficult. "Then obey and be still."

Or another lesson would take place.

"Return to where you were standing." He snapped his fingers and pointed to the space before him. "This is the only warning I am going to give. Do not back away from me again."

She crept forward, hunched like a broken doll, and let the man's hands go where they would.

Unlike Esin, Uriel was not interested in tweaking her nipples or palming her ass. His movements were perfunctory, his objective simple: teaching her how to put on the *real dress*.

Once the scandalous blue garment was back in place, he said, "You have questions, Morgaine, and are encouraged to ask them. My duty is to answer them as clearly and honestly as I can. What is coming will be difficult for you if you do not take this opportunity to heart. Remember that. Do not waste your time on hysterics."

"Coming for me?" Penetration? Subjugation? Humiliation? What else did these monsters have in store? Hysterics seem the natural reaction to this nightmare.

"I will make you a plate of food." He took her elbow, leading her to the table where she'd been sick. "As you eat, we will talk."

Sitting where she was directed, Morgaine tried to make that *dress* cover as much as possible.

The vomit on the table Sergeant Uriel covered with a nearby napkin, picking through the foodstuffs on display to arrange a plate of simple bread and nuts. When it was before her, he cocked his head for her to eat, and said, "In Corporal Esin's presence, slick dripped from your cunt. What followed upset you."

Cunt? That was the most vulgar word Morgaine knew. No one spoke it casually while wiping up cold vomit with a silk napkin.

So she kept her mouth shut and her eyes on the plate.

Silence seemed the answer Sergeant Uriel desired. As if to reward her restraint, a soft purr filled the air between them. "This transition is only as difficult as you make it."

She nodded, picking at a piece of bread.

It had been only a few hours since she'd woken. Many things had been said, much of it out of her understanding. There were words thrown around she'd never heard, insinuations, expectations... none of it clear. Daring to glace up from her plate, she met the sergeant's eyes and asked, "Why am I here if not to be punished?"

"Eat three more bites." He waited as she did so, stoic yet continuing to purr. When the last of her food was swallowed down, he said, "You are here to be made whole."

Taking her by the elbow again, he led her to the center of the room She was made to sit on a bench facing the forest view. "Keep your eyes on the screen.

When I return, we will discuss what you've learned. Do not make me describe what will happen should you disobey."

HER HAIR HAD DRIED, her skin was dry, but the cushion under her body was saturated with unwelcome, slippery fluid. Little puddles collected on the floor where liquid dripped from the bench or ran down in rivulets over calves and bare feet.

The air in the room was drenched in an unusual sweet scent.

Slick, as Sergeant Uriel had called it, seasoned every breath.

No matter how she tried to will it away, she could not stop more from leaking.

And she had tried. Bunching up the front panel of her skirt and pressing it between her legs had not helped. The fabric had grown soaked, and now stuck to her skin in a way that made her want to remove it completely.

Every inch where the blue gown clung felt itchy, so itchy, that had she been back in her cottage, she would have torn the damn thing off and let the air play against her skin instead.

These unnatural feelings and thoughts, Morgaine

understood where they come from. It was the wall before her, alive again with provocative images.

And she had been told to sit and pay attention.

The things displayed were vulgar in nature, though little could be seen beyond a pretty girl's expression and the bunching musculature of the male's back who pinned her down. It was more the story told in lascivious groans and coarse grunts as that unseen man surged forward, over and over. The Alpha's every sound was obscene, the volume turned up to echo loudly throughout Morgaine's room. The girl the Omega projected on the wall, her eager moans and keen cries were even louder.

Like Esmerelda's, the unnamed female's irises had been eaten up fully by a black pupil. Only this time, Morgaine had watched the transformation from honey-eyed innocent, to black-eyed... she was not even sure what to call such a wanton female. Whore?

The male called her mate. And then he had growled at her until the woman was practically salivating.

It was not a noise that inspired lust upon the room's solo audience. The Alpha's growl had been animalistic and dangerous, similar in tone to the low-pitched rumble that had come from Esin when he'd pawed her body earlier.

She had hated the sound of it... yet against her

will, it had inspired a fresh rush of slick to warm her thighs.

When the Alpha on screen had pushed *his mate* down, Morgaine had been unable to see what made the girl squeal. All she could see was the look on the Omega's face, and how her breath had caught with that first sharp surge.

The beast used her roughly and for an extended period of time, until the girl was screaming for release, until even Morgaine had dug her fingernails into her palms in anticipation of this thing she'd only heard whispered about between the girls back home.

And then the roar.

It shook the room, shook Morgaine, and left the place between her legs clenching around a sorry feeling of emptiness.

She even whimpered, her nipples growing so tight they throbbed.

"He is knotting her now, the base of his member expanding inside her body as he ejaculates."

Distracted by lewd images, the pulsing, plumped flesh between her legs, and the unrelenting itch to rub the ache from her breasts, she'd not heard Sergeant Uriel return. Eyes wide, she darted a glance over her shoulder, embarrassed to be seen in such a state.

There was no way to hide her drenched lap, the puddles, where her hands had wandered… the smell.

Smell? Yes there was a delightful smell. Nostrils

flaring, she took in a deep breath. Musk… rich spiced skin. Sweat.

Like a starving woman, she closed her eyes as she savored the taste on her tongue.

"If you were to look at yourself right now, Morgaine, you would find your eyes mirror the Omega in the image. Your pupils are blown, your cunt has grown ripe and ushers slick. Both reactions entice an Alpha into the rut. Were you in estrous, like the Omega on the screen, they would be compounded, and you would be begging any male to ease your excitement. You would be unable to stop yourself."

"Estrous?"

He nodded. "An uncontrolled estrous was the reason Esmeralda and all the settlers died. Her body's pheromones instigated a rut Beta males could not resist. She died. They died. Everyone suffered. Yet in a controlled environment, in the care of an experienced Alpha, estrous brings great pleasure."

Staring, glassy-eyed, Morgaine unknowingly licked her lips, yet openly disagreed. "I would not beg."

The corner of Uriel's mouth turned up, the fine lines beside his eyes charming. "Your pride is something to be seen, girl. It has caught the attention of several Alphas and complicated arbitration. Many desire you for a mate."

Mate?

Like the male on the wall? The one holding her down and making the loud Omega squeal?

Just the thought had her breasts grow heavy and sore. Unthinking, she reached up to soothe them. Once her palms were full of flesh, the outrageousness of her behavior began to register. Caught mindlessly groping herself in front of this…Alpha, she blinked once, snapped out of it, and put a hand over her mouth in shame.

Uriel attempted to placate. "I am not offended by your interest. You responded to the exercise exactly as you should have. And if you wish to partake, I can send a suitable Alpha in to guide you through sexual stimulation to orgasm."

To be pushed down and entered as the Omega on the screen had been? Just the thought made her pussy clench with such power, fluid rushed from between her legs to splatter on the floor.

Never had a Beta's attentions inspired her lust.

And lust is all this was.

Lust was an empty, hollow emotion that, when indulged in, left a person sullied. Love was what was required.

Love was the reason women in her settlement went to great lengths to keep their modesty intact. Suitors were not to be tempted by their bodies, but by their deeds and their minds.

Yet she was very much caught in the tempting

throes of lust. All of this from watching one pair grunting on the screen.

And she had not even seen them fucking... she'd only seen the Alpha's back and the Omega's face.

Perhaps her horrid neighbor had been right. She was a harlot.

Her eyes left the Alpha, traveling to feast upon the fur scraps in the sunken bed. A whisper of so much softness against her skin; that would cool this heat. She could sprawl about that nest, roll around and luxuriate like a cat. Find what she needed.

Uriel purred temptation with a voice of pure velvet. "An experienced Alpha is waiting right outside the door, Morgaine. Shall I let him in?"

A stranger in a strange room who would touch her in an odd sunken bed saturated by the scent of many males. Why that sounded delicious, she could not say.

"It could be more than one Alpha. Do you wish to sample those with the greatest stake in claiming you as theirs? They would spoil you."

Multiple males?

Esmeralda had died horribly being savaged by multiple males. Her murder had been a sad, frightening thing.

Fear sobered her.

As if he saw the change, Uriel increased the sound of his purr. "They would be gentle, Morgaine. Exceedingly careful."

Esin had not been gentle when he'd grabbed her arm and forced it from her breasts. He had not been gentle when he'd wrapped her fingers around his cock and jerked her fist up and down.

Had they been exceedingly careful when they'd held her mother against the wall by her neck? How about when they branded that sweet woman's face? Were the Alphas careful in that?

This whole situation was absurd.

In one day, she'd woken in fear, watched a gruesome death, been pawed by a male she despised, ordered around, and covered in semen. Her life was in the hands of Alpha soldiers she could not see—men who manipulated the very room they had trapped her in so she might bend to their will. She had no say. Instead, she was told that she would want everything they had planned for her. And then she had become aroused to the point of insanity by nothing more than images on a wall.

This was not who she was. Her reputation in the settlement was excellent. Morgaine was a steady girl, one who could weave cloth almost as fine as her mother's.

Her mother... who was alone in their cottage. And she would never see her again. One outlandish projection on the wall could not take away that heartache.

Sexual excitement faded into hopelessness, the change in her scent obvious to them both.

Wretched, Morgaine muttered, "I bet she's sitting on my cot, right now, crying into my pillow. And unlike myself, I doubt she has eaten anything today. What has been done will destroy her, and there is nothing I can do but sit here and *obey*."

"The Beta female was well compensated for her beautiful Omega offspring. She will never have to work again... might even have enough to tempt a settler of standing into taking her as wife. She could have more children, Beta children she could keep."

Morgaine scoffed outright. "Alphas ruined her future long ago. No settler would have her. It was bad enough that one of you put me in her body, only for another Alpha to take me away. I was her everything... and you burned her face for protecting me from the same fate you forced on her."

Narrowing his eyes, measuring her words, body language, and anger, Uriel grew unnervingly silent.

Angry over what had been done to her, what had been done to her mother, and that she had no way to fix any of it, Morgaine threw in his face, "You didn't know? Is it against your code to use Beta women when you come to rob us?" Slinging the newest word in her vocabulary with spite, Morgaine grew mean. "You only *mount* Omegas?"

A measured answer was offered despite her outright rudeness. "If what you say is confirmed, the Alpha in question will face great penalties. Betas are protected—we assure they never suffer disease, hunger, or war. Alphas design, supply, and protect their Eden, and in exchange we take what's owed."

"Protect from what?" She pointed at him, all the unspent lust twisting into spite. "The only thing we have to fear is you."

Her words set off the musk of Alpha anger. Gritting his teeth, Sergeant Uriel growled, "You have no idea the dangers in this universe. I cannot count the Alphas who have sacrificed their lives so you might flourish in peace. There is war even now, always war, that you, your mother, your people have all been shielded from. Be grateful, and consider why we take Omegas while they are still young. The love you feel for your mother was stolen. It was stolen from your future mate. It belongs to him alone, and he will help you learn that."

"Then I hate him already." Turning her head to dismiss the intruder, Morgaine made herself look at the lovers' continued ecstasy, and ignored the feeling of more slick trickling down her leg.

6

Wrinkling her nose, Morgaine went back to her silent rebellion. A night had passed in that unnatural room. There had been clear instructions on where and how to sleep. Any rest outside the nest would be considered insubordination.

They had left her little choice in the matter.

After supper, Sergeant Uriel had wrestled her out of her garment and left her naked in a shrieking pile on the floor.

"There is no shame in nudity, girl." He stood over her, stern, huge, and less than impressed to see more tears. "You are beautiful. Your mate will take great joy in seeing you this way."

Shins to the ground, forehead tucked to her knees, Morgaine kept her arms wrapped around her skull.

She wouldn't be moved, refused to let another male see her unclothed. Tucked into a ball of rage, phrases so unseemly she would have earned a slap even from her sweet mother vomited into the air.

"I cannot allow you to keep the dress and foster a misrepresentation of what to expect once bonded. You are here to learn." He sounded so calm, so collected, that it enraged her all the more. "Neither Omega or Alpha sleep clothed when in their den. It's unnatural."

There was no getting through to the exhausted woman. "I hate you all! GET OUT!"

The lecture continued as if she were sitting prim before him, not in the midst of a meltdown at his feet. "Many Omegas find it more comfortable to remain unclothed the first few years once mated. Not only is it practical, it is considered an act of affection to preen for their Alpha."

Her screams turned to silent seething.

"You will sleep now. *In the nest.* You will burrow and use the furs for warmth." When she refused to move, the grainy nature of his words rolled ominously, and the sergeant's purr dried up. "If you refuse the comfort of your nest, the consequences will be severe and painful. I will not have you abuse yourself in an effort to be difficult."

Sensing that he was reaching down, Morgaine used the last of her raw voice to hiss, "If you so much as lay a finger on me, I will bite you!"

"That is an unwise threat to level at an Alpha." His hand settled between her shoulder blades, firmly planted when she flinched. "A bite from an Omega is something we enjoy. Though my mate would be jealous should I return to her with the marks of your teeth on my flesh."

That was all it took, that small hint of mockery to bat aside the last of her slipping sanity.

Not even her teeth could threaten them. She had nothing. No possible way off their ship. No idea where in the universe she might be. She didn't even grasp how the wall became a door.

It sank in slowly while she lay draped over her knees on the floor.

They could do whatever they wanted to her… and they were going to.

They were going to give her clothes only to take them away. They were going to use her hands for their pleasure. They were going to rape her.

No sudden rampage came with cold acceptance, no quickly flung out hand to claw his face. Morgaine only grew silent and still, staring forward and seeing nothing.

"Now, go to bed, Morgaine."

Not so much as a blink was offered, Morgaine lost in a mental retreat.

So he dragged her like a sullen child to the

sleeping pit, the Omega offering no protest when he laid her down.

She offered no life at all.

He organized her limbs. Kneeling at her side, he scooped up the fur scraps and dumped them over her body for warmth. Sergeant Uriel even used the flat of his hand to brush her unblinking eyes closed. "This transition is only as difficult as you make it, child."

Was it child now? What happened to girl? How about Omega?

Why had he never once called her woman?

She was of age, possessed all the skills a woman of standing must know. She had even been courted *properly* by a few young men from the settlement. Every last one of them had heeded her refusal like a man. With dignity and kindness.

Even smarmy Hanna's boy, Cassius, had only moped for a few days.

Alpha males were the childish ones with their demands and threats if they didn't get their way. Yet she was the one lying flopped over the cushions of the sleeping pit like a disgruntled toddler.

It wouldn't do.

How many painful cycles had she weathered when the Alphas came? Dozens. She had borne excruciating pain far more graciously than this. She had endured. She had survived.

She was not a child.

Sniffing, she'd sat up in the dark and let out a troubled sigh.

The room had grown freezing again, the stinking furs offering her only source of warmth. Toying with a piece, she absently ran the soft white fluff back and forth under her fingers.

They wanted her to sleep, but they could not force her.

The could force her body, but they could not bend her mind.

Take away everything, clothes, comfort, safety… but her knowledge and years of experience would always be with her—her weapons in this cold, dark place. And she wanted them to know that.

In the small hours, trapped in a freezing, dark room that stank of men she'd never met, she made a stand.

Like any industrious woman born in a settlement, she knew how to skin, stretch, and cure a beast's hide. She knew how to prepare it into fine edging for garments and how to line winter clothing for warmth.

Alas, sewing fur required a sturdy needle and thread, two things she did not have. But tearing the edges of soft hide and tying the strips together would bind two pieces just as well. And plenty of fur had been provided.

Under the cover of dark, she worked the scraps of soft fur, ignoring the scent tickling her nostrils. Hour after hour, her fingers grew swollen and stiff from the effort it took to tear hide. She didn't care, for when her fingers blistered, she used her teeth. As diligent as she would have been over her loom, she grabbed at random bits, rent, tied, knotting segments into panels, until she had enough to cover her nakedness. The faster she worked, the more sloppy her creation grew, fatigue and desperation warring within her body.

When morning came and Sergeant Uriel stepped through that impossible wall, he found her dressing in a mangled fur wrap she was still building around her. Red-rimmed eyes were unwilling to glance up from her work to address him.

"What is the meaning of this?" The Alpha's question was not aggressive, nor did it carry the weight of imminent punishment. It was merely inquisitive.

Dry lips parted, Morgaine muttering to herself as if lost in a spell. In all of it, only four words made sense. "…I am no child."

"Put it down, Morgaine."

Clutching the furs to her chest, she peeled her lips in a snarl and growled. The low uneven rumble, warned of a cornered beast willing to harm itself to harm the other. "You told me to sleep under the furs."

Bedraggled, eyes sunken, and skin sallow, it was obvious she had not slept at all. The Alpha chose to contemplate, standing at a distance long enough that the Omega went back to tearing and tying, tearing and tying, over and over until she'd gone through all the fur.

When it was complete and there was no more work for her reddened hands, he asked, "And what is it you intend to do with that now?"

Pulling the garment tighter around her body, she ignored the Alpha-stink, and stared forward. "Be warm."

Stepping into her pit, armored boots distorting the cushions, Sergeant Uriel towered over her. "You were ordered to sleep."

She blinked, silent and victorious.

"And yet you spend your hours slotted for rest making *that*." He gestured to her garment, brow furrowing, and displeasure growing obvious. "Did you think I'd allow you to keep it? That I would not see through this little rebellion?"

Meeting his stone cold gaze, she held her covering all the tighter.

"Now you shall have no dress when Corporal Esin arrives to see to your grooming."

For such a small exhausted thing, she was remarkably fast in scrambling out from under his legs and fleeing across the room.

"You will unknot every last piece of fur you damaged with your antics." He made a dash after her, boots loud yet voice unnervingly mellow. "Every last piece, Morgaine."

Rounding the table, fur skirt caught up in her hands, she evaded again.

No breath was wasted on argument, not when her legs were wobbling and her arms tired from hours of labor. She just continued to run.

But he was so much larger, a hunter, a soldier, and she was only a frightened... *child.* A child far from her settlement with absolutely no way of ever returning, who wanted nothing more in the world than her mother.

It was her own garment that brought an end to the game of cat and mouse. She tripped on the long skirt and went sprawling, chin hitting the floor with enough force to knock her senseless.

Stars still spun in her vision when Sergeant Uriel turned her over, cursing loudly. He pinned her to the frosty floor, though she was too senseless to properly struggle. Whether it was lack of air from the weight of his boot that sent her spiraling into unconsciousness, or just too many hours of unconscionable anxiety, Morgaine fell into a painful sleep that brought with it no rest.

When she woke, she was back in the sleeping pit, Corporal Esin half-dressed at her side—the man unknotting her dress one bit at a time.

Chest bare, he didn't seem at all happy with the task of stripping her. In fact, he met her eyes and let her see a man full of heartache. "You shouldn't have done it, renegade."

She tried to flop away, to give him her back, but found her leg was caught under a heavy thigh.

"Silence will not make this any easier."

Jaw aching, she parted her teeth and grimaced at the sharp sting of pain. Hand to her face, testing the bone, she found the slip of medicinal unguent coated her chin.

"You're lucky your jaw is intact."

What an outrageous concept. "Lucky?"

Attempting to brush a tangle of hair from her forehead, Esin seemed surprised when she jumped and shoved his hand away. "I'm not here to hurt you."

The building pressure behind her eyes, the constant throb in her skull, were made all the worse from simple movement. Groaning, she sank back into the pillows, glaring at her tormentor.

He tried again, hand moving slowly, to lift the tangled lock and tuck it behind her ear. "As I said, I have no wish to hurt you. Ever. I bore the brunt of your punishment myself, because I cannot bear to see you in pain."

He turned at the waist so she might look upon the damage done to his back. Crusted lines of open skin still oozed. "Three stripes."

Her actions had caused him pain? This was a victory indeed. "I hope it hurts a great deal."

Smiling as if her callousness was cute, Esin tried to cuddle closer. It did not go as he would have hoped. She tore at her furs, at him, at the bedding in a useless attempt to be free.

And was easily caught.

Whispering a secret, he ignored her thrashing and began picking at a new knot. "I was taken from my mother too, you know. It was a long time ago, but I do remember missing her. That is our way of life, our laws… our tenets that lead to fulfilment and happiness. We all have our place. Yours is with your Alpha, where you will be loved and spoiled."

"And when that Alpha fills me with a child, how long before it's taken from me?"

He paused to consider, weighing his reply in a way that prompted Morgaine's suspicion. "Your offspring would reside and train on this ship. I could do that for you if it would make you happy."

"You cannot imagine that any life you paint for me would be one I want. You stole me from the life I wanted. You burned my mother's face. There is not a single male on this ship I would ever be happy to…"

"Fuck?"

Her skin crawled just seeing the way his eyes burned speaking that word.

More of his weight came to pin her down, Corporal Esin grinning. "Come now, feisty renegade.

You make the challenge so much sweeter when you look at me that way. I do love to hunt."

"Get off of me!"

"My orders are to strip you of this *thing*, and teach you to accept touch. You will be denied clothing today. I will play with you, then you will be groomed. To show you that your comfort is paramount, I will not use your mouth until your jaw has healed."

7

She never landed so much as a blow.

Thighs shaking, she bore his weight, unable to do more than croak. Throat burning as if she'd swallowed shards of glass, she'd given up on speech, and lay limp just as he desired.

His purr was incessant, conflicting with the random growls he pressed against her throat. Pulled back and forth between the two manipulative noises, she'd grown listless and edgy, angry and sullen, but mostly tired and pained by the position.

"Do you feel where I am touching you? There are nerves here, renegade, whose only purpose is sexual pleasure." He groaned as he stroked, teasing at a throbbing nubbin of flesh at the apex of her sex.

There was no pleasure in being held down, or screaming until one's voice was lost.

"You are producing slick," Esin's voice caught, Morgaine certain he was holding on by a thread. The man had already sucked his fingers clean more times than she could count, mmmming over them as his eyes rolled back.

And then he had gathered up more of that awful substance, scooping it from between her legs to smear over her breasts.

He'd licked it all off, nipping so hard in places she'd been marked.

The purr faltered. Esin growled again. And another bead of slick seeped.

He stroked her clitoris faster, Morgaine certain the little bunch of flesh would soon be worn away.

It hurt.

The zings, the tingles… they were not pleasant.

Not like this.

"Once you come, I'll stop. Give me that, renegade. Give me your pleasure."

Faster his fingers flew, centering on that same spot until raw skin began to sting. Her insides clenched in a defiant cramp, twisted, made her retch, and finally released.

If this was sex, it was horrible.

Panting, Morgaine was forced to look into the ecstatic face of the male responsible for such discomfort.

"Good girl." He sniffed at her neck, clearly

thrilled she'd practically thrown up on him. "I'd love nothing more than to lick you clean, but I don't trust myself. My cock already aches." He set her hands free, gathering one so he might draw it between them. He ran her fingers through her oversensitive slick-coated folds and then smeared his bared cock with her touch. "Go on now, like I showed you last time."

He was going to make her lay like this, under him and spread while he used her hand? Hips already aching, she tried to rock her body, to get blood back into her joints.

"No, no. No fucking today." A grisly chuckle paired with a nuzzle of her cheek, and words that made her skin crawl. "Do not try to tempt me. I've taken enough lashes to keep a clear head no matter how pretty you are or how sweet you smell. Rub my cock like a good girl, and maybe I'll pleasure you twice before your bath."

The skin between her legs was on fire, if he tried to touch her there again, she'd…

What would she do? Cry until there were no more tears? Scream until her voice was nothing more than a wheeze?

What had that gained her?

Her hand around his organ hardly moved. It didn't need to. Esin was pumping his hips into her sorry grip. Positioned as he was, it was mimicry of penetration— his thrusts angling the head of his cock to skim her mound and belly. Jerked by his movements, gaping at his screwed up face, there was little she could do but brace and hope it ended quickly.

"Take your hand." He was straining, the veins in his neck popping against twitching muscle. "Grip the base of my cock and squeeze."

What?

"Now! Do it now!"

A bulge was beginning to grow near the thatch of hair at his groin. Swelling, it distorted his shaft like a growing cancer.

"Gahhh!" He took matters into his own hand, forcing her fist down and squeezing their joined touch so tight her finger joints popped. Surging upright, his free hand began to milk his cock furiously until a fat glob of thick goop erupted to land on her stomach.

It was the first of many.

So much surged from the man it was mind boggling—breasts, stomach, chest, and thighs were coated to dripping.

And still Esin wasn't done. Teeth clenched he hissed, "Don't let go. DON'T LET GO!"

"You're hurting my wrist…" The words were but a breath, Morgaine's arm shaking in her attempt to dislodge herself from his grip.

What started out thick became a spray of warm rain. It lacked the pearly quality of the first abundant spillage, and dripped like water down her skin. With the burst came a roar from the man who glared down to watch his prize squirm in all he showered upon her.

"Open your mouth."

No. Never.

"Just a taste, renegade." He chided, teasing at her lips with his glans. "Drink up what I offer."

Fiercely shaking her head, Morgaine went from trying to pull away to pushing against him.

Whatever that did to his knot made him keen, buck his hips and spray her with another volley of musky fluid, until it gummed in her lashes and matted her hair.

Esin kept her this way, stuck beneath him, for the entire duration that bulbous growth at the base of his angry, red cock persisted.

The breaks between his subsequent orgasms led to him kneading his knot and her fingers so hard she began to lose feeling. In that span, he spoke to her of how best to drain him. What a great job she had done for her first time milking a knot. But he also admonished her refusal to part her lips.

Had her jaw not been damaged, she was sure he would have forced her teeth apart and jammed that hideous thing down her throat.

Four more times, semen shot out as he groaned, arched, and spoke filth to the ceiling.

The final eruption was little more than a dribble of

clear fluid that ran down their joined hands to trickle between them.

Setting her throbbing hand free with a filthy groan, Esin rubbed at the diminishing knot until his cock grew flaccid. With his flesh appeased, he fell back down upon her, laughing at her breathy attempt to squeal as he used his naked chest to rub his semen into her skin.

"Mine." Over and over he muttered the lie. "All mine."

She was not his.

She was more than a hand, or a body to taste.

She was greater than the nub of flesh between her legs he felt was so important.

And so she told herself, while rough hands slipped and slid over places that man's come should have been allowed to pool.

"They will be so pleased with you, renegade. No Omega has ever made me jettison seven times." Kissing her mouth so hard his teeth knocked hers, Esin cooed. "Seven… you dirty girl. And look at you: perfect with my come flavoring your lips."

Pulling back enough she might draw a desperate breath, Esin teased, *"Perfectly disobedient*, I should say. I told you to open your mouth and you refused…"

Pressing her lips tight, Morgaine looked away.

The taste of him had already migrated to her mouth, but she would not invite more of it.

"Disobedience must be punished. There will be no more pleasure for you today. Think on that while we bathe." He went back to toying with the drying fluids on her skin, fingers tripping over ribs and navel. "I would have left you very satisfied. Now I will leave you dripping slick and hungry for my attention."

She let out a quick sigh of relief—one that was mistaken by her tormentor as regret.

Face suddenly serious, he took her aching chin, turning her head so she might meet his eyes. "A good, rough finger fuck is for obedient Omegas who don't destroy their furs and open their mouths for their Alpha. Next time I come to tend you, remember how you feel right now."

Morgaine would remember, and Morgaine would keep her lips sealed.

"Will you give me a kiss?"

Another head shake.

"Pouting, eh?" Laughing deeply, Esin offered a hint of purr in an attempt to placate his toy. "That is no way to convince me to pet my pretty girl's pussy."

Walking his fingers down her body, he made to reach between her thighs, stopped only by the sound of water filling the tub.

"It looks as if we've played too long." Rolling off her at last, he moved with all the jovial energy Morgaine lacked. He even snorted playfully as he drew her to her feet. "More like they found me too lenient and wanted us out of the nest. Punishment is punishment."

Her legs were numb and she wobbled, caught up by the smiling man who winked. "You already have me wrapped around your finger."

No AMOUNT of bathing might make her feel clean—though Esin took great pains to make sure he lathered her in every possible place as she sat in his lap. It was the first bath she'd been forced to share, and though he had soaped his semen from her skin, the purpose of the bath was not her pleasure, but his.

He was there to instruct her how to tend to an Alpha.

Hands still gnarled and raw from the making of her ruined fur covering, still aching from how hard he'd squeezed her against his knot, she was made to knead his shoulders. Straddling his lap, face to face in a way that felt disturbingly intimate, he coaxed her to take the soap and learn to touch him in the way men liked best.

His groans when he tossed his head back at her touch did not warm the heart. His almost gentle caress of her hips under the water did not ease her mind.

Fondly, he purred, a content mass of muscle that demanded to be stroked. Eyes shining, a lazy smile on his face, he said, "You really are beautiful. Perfect, just like I said the first time I saw you."

When his cohort had her mother's neck in his hands, threatening to burn her alive.

"I don't want to think of that." Not while she was being forced to groom the male responsible.

"I understood you." Catching her lower lip with his thumb, Esin shook his head. He sounded far less happy when he added, "One day you will remember that moment in another light. It will have been the first time you saw the mate you adore."

Loath maybe? Voice like sandpaper, she continued to run her hands in lazy circles over his shoulders like directed. "You are not my mate."

Stern, he tensed, undoing all her hard work to soften his mass. "I will go to any length to ensure that I will be."

Morgaine chose not to answer, reaching instead for more soap.

"You don't believe me?"

She believed that she was trapped on a nameless ship, god only knew where in space, surrounded by the enemy. An enemy who had just done disgusting things to her… again.

It turned out she had more tears after all.

They began to fall, her shoulders shaking with the effort to bite back painful sobs.

Esin took pity on the overwhelmed Omega,

pulling her tight to his chest. At her stiff resistance, an intense purr came from him, vibrating so close to her body she felt it rattle her bones.

The heat of his hands rose from the water. They ran over the musculature of her back, kneading too hard to be considered comfortable. Esin would find a knot and attack it while she hissed through the pain. Over long minutes, muscles released.

He touched with intent, lips at her ear as he described how greatly her softness pleased him. Telling her how comfortable her future would be. She would want for nothing. Never go hungry. Never suffer loneliness as he had while waiting to find her.

In time she went limp.

Breath soft at her ear, he asked, "Is that better?"

A raspy croak complained, "I'm hungry."

"Good." Her sullen words drew him to hold her a little tighter. "I brought you food I had specially prepared. A gift we might enjoy together before I must depart for duty."

8

───────

Though Esin seemed optimistic with Morgaine's behavior, Sergeant Uriel continued to press for a rapid and drastic change.

When he had come to see her upon Esin's retreat, he shared none of the lower-ranking male's smiles.

One sniff of the nest told a story Esin either failed to notice, or discounted out of pride.

But the astringent sting in the air spoke of much more than fear. It spoke of revulsion, of shame…

Even with direct stimulation, Morgaine failed to respond as expected. He climbed into her nest, unsettled the furs, sniffing often and growled in a ceaseless low hum of displeasure.

Damaged.

He might have muttered it under his breath, but she'd heard.

Maybe she was broken, but better to be broken than a mindless Alpha puppet. Standing where the sergeant had told her to wait, Morgaine watched him grow openly agitated. Before she might earn a lesson, she pleaded her defense. "I did everything he wanted."

The sergeant's slipping tolerance was been replaced with antagonism. Snapping his attention from the inadequate nest to her face, his voice came rough, angry and unforgiving. "Not only did he refrain from penetrating you for your comfort, he saw to your pleasure before his own." Frustrated with her utter unwillingness to allow Corporal Esin to so much as smell the air around her without stinking of fear, impatient with her anger, her pleading, and her disgust, Uriel climbed from the nest, marching forward to stand over her and accuse. "I watched you enjoy it."

It was uncanny knowing strangers had watched her scream at the top of her lungs, careless of how raw her voice had become when Esin began to rip off her furs. Morgaine had bit and scratched until sound failed her completely. She had cried for her mother when he'd forced open her legs.

The effort was for nothing.

Drawing her arms protectively around her body, Morgaine found she could not meet his gaze. She had felt unseen eyes on her from the first moments in this pretty prison—the lights, the tub, the cold air that would blast about as if there had been a change in the false forest's wind… the images on the wall. All were coordinated by whomever was tasked with monitoring her.

Her blood like ice, Morgaine said aloud what they all knew, certain every move she made had been projected for strangers to witness all these days of her captivity, "You watched?"

"Of course." Sergeant Uriel pointed at the artificial view of the forest on the screen that had previously shown the death of Esmerelda and the mating of the estrous-high Omega. "Beyond that wall, many Alphas observe your every move. There is a team in place to regulate your keeping and assure your happiness. Many among them are your suitors who have a legal right to have proof you are honored."

Honored? If Uriel was frustrated, Morgaine was exasperated.

Love, happiness, safety, joy, pleasure—these words had been barked at her over and over, but never *once* had she felt any of them in Alpha care. Honor did not exist here.

He wasn't done. "Furthermore, all mated Omegas are broadcast in their finest moments. How else are Alphas to learn how to please them, care for them, and discipline them where there are so few to go around? Grow accustomed to being watched."

Amazed these monsters had found another way to shock her, Morgaine's jaw dropped. "You allow other men to view your mate during..."

Pride swelling his chest, Sergeant Uriel stood tall. He even dared a hit of a smile. "Alphas need release. If they can find pleasure in the same moment I do, then it is my duty to provide it. An undrained Alpha is dangerous."

"She is comfortable with this?"

"Like you, she has no choice." He seemed to consider as if the thought had never occurred to him, following with, "I believe she takes delight in doing her duty for both me and the crew."

Cheeks fiery red as the concept sunk in, she dared to meet the Alpha's eyes. "Have you asked her?"

"Why would I?"

It was such a flippant reply that Morgaine could not help but snarl, "Because you love her... Because sex is sacred? Because even now I feel as if it was more than Esin who violated me."

He gave her a slap, hard enough to sting, but not rough enough to knock her down. "Grasp this. You cannot be raped by an Alpha. You are an Omega, designed by nature to respond to our call."

Hand to her stinging cheek, Morgaine stumbled back. "I did what he wanted..."

Countering her wobbly retreat, the sergeant came down upon her until she'd tripped and fallen hard on her rear. Reeking of furious Alpha musk, he roared. "You spent half the experience screaming for your mother! You are lucky he chose to exercise patience and leniency! Had it been I, you would have been silenced with that first embarrassing bleat!"

There was nothing to do but try to shrink back and appease, her every synapse warned that she was in danger. "I'm sorry."

Seething, he closed his eyes, took a breath, and slowly grew collected. When a full minute had passed, he nodded at a thought, became the meditative man she'd first met, and said, "You'll be silenced now. One more mention of her in any context, Morgaine, and there will be three strikes of the cane for you and a public whipping for Elizabeta where all your settlement might watch."

Stricken, Morgaine could mutter no more than a terrified. "No..."

"Yes." He seemed proud of the decree. "You will learn discipline. The best you can do for your mother is to forget she ever existed. Slip up, and she will bleed far more than you will. Someday you will even thank me for breaking you of your childish habit."

His threat had set Morgaine into uncontrollable sobs no amount of purring could ease. Her punishment she could bear, but knowing her mother, a woman who was already grieving and in pain, would be whipped, could never be borne.

"Think on all I've said." Uriel kneeled down and placed a hand on her bowed, shaking head. "Tomorrow you will impress me with the behavior of a woman and not the poor conduct of a child."

He'd left her alone to cry it out. The lights had gone down and she had dumped herself into the sunken bed far away from the reeking furs and crusting remnants of Esin's semen.

Hopeless and exhausted, she lay as still as a corpse no matter the artificial chill they pushed into the air.

They had taken her from her home. They had forced her to watch unspeakable things, made demands that were degrading and repugnant. And now… now they wanted to take her mother's name out of her mouth.

It was worse than being stolen away, because Morgaine knew that one day *she would slip*. One day she would mention her mother, and the woman who loved her above all things would pay dearly for it.

WHEN THE LIGHTS CAME UP, it had been after another sleepless night.

Sergeant Uriel entered with renewed vigor. Professional, with none of the prior day's harsh temperament, he said, "I see you've spent a great deal of time in thought."

Too tired to do anything but nod, Morgaine remained silent. Silence, in fact, was the best she could manage from now on. They wanted someone who only spoke when addressed. Now they would have one. Otherwise conversation would ignite a constant state of anxiety. It would be too easy to make a mistake.

Every phrase must be measured so that single, beautiful word might never pass her lips.

"Well, girl." He cocked a brow. "Tell me your thoughts."

Her thoughts were the most dangerous topic and would never be mentioned again. Rubbing her lips together, formulating an admissible reply, she said, "It's time for breakfast."

This displeased Sergeant Uriel. "Describe your distress."

"I'm hungry."

Lower went his unconvinced brow. "What is wrong with you?"

"I didn't sleep well."

"Enough, Omega." He marched to where she stood meek and submissive just as he'd trained her. "You will explain this temperament."

The more he pushed, the more Morgaine grew certain it was all some test. If she were to slip and explain a single thought in her head, she would fail.

And her mother would be mercilessly beaten.

He was waiting for an answer and she needed to find an appropriate one. A half-truth was the best she could do. "I have a slight headache."

In fact, her head was pounding.

"My Omega enjoys when I brush her hair." The locks that had modestly covered her bare breasts were gathered, Sergeant Uriel rubbing the golden waves between his fingers. "Would you enjoy such attention?"

Another test? "Does an Alpha enjoy offering it?"

"There is a deep satisfaction earned in pleasing one's mate."

Back in the settlement, after long days laboring over a loom, her mother would comb out her hair—offering her only child comfort, compassion, and love. The manipulation of large male hands wouldn't erase the memory, only make it more painful. "Then I would be expected to comply."

"That is an unsatisfactory answer, Morgaine."

Anxiety bubbled into depression. Silent tears fell, Morgaine afraid if he heard her so much as sniff, a lesson would follow. "I don't have a mate to comb out my hair, so I cannot answer you."

"Do you want a mate?"

She wanted her mother. Eyes red, sinuses swollen, she stared forward and strove to be obedient. "You say a mate will make me feel happy. Everyone wants to be happy."

"What's wrong, Morgaine?"

She shook her head and did what Sergeant Uriel had told her was her purpose. "Nothing. What would you like me to do next?"

He wiped her tears, gentle in action but stern in voice. "Stop crying."

Quiet, she nodded… and failed.

The wet drips kept falling.

With a resigned sigh, the sergeant dropped his hands from her hair and took a step away. "This will not do, Omega."

Scrubbing her cheeks with the back of her hand, Morgaine sniffed. "I'm trying. I swear it."

"And I believe you." Abandoning her to her mood, he moved away. "Eat. I will return later."

With that last word, he disappeared, leaving her a whole day alone to sit with her thoughts. The time was spent instead in dark, dreamless sleep.

9

Half buried under the scented furs, Morgaine barely stirred when Uriel burst in for the next day's work.

His demeanor had altered drastically. Pensive agitation was gone, fresh determination behind his words instead. "We knew you would be feral, but having analyzed your complaints, we agree you are also under the false impression that you are not safe or cared for by our strict standards."

Pacing back and forth, he spoke as if addressing soldiers at attention. "Every law has been followed. Every rule exacted with precision to ease your adjustment."

Rubbing her eyes, Morgaine sat up with all the enthusiasm of a woman about to be fed to lions.

Appraising the unenthusiastic bend of her spine,

he paused his march. He even bore the look of regret. "I cannot provide what you require. As such, there is only one recourse. Your belligerent temperament has altered the timeline for the selection of your mate."

Unmoved, almost unfeeling, Morgaine asked, "Who?"

Coming to stand at the edge of the sleeping pit, Uriel frowned down upon the sad scene—an Omega who refused the comforts offered. "Despite your protests, I will no longer deny suitors from their rightful turn for physical interaction. Corporal Esin holds the greatest claim, he shall be first. Penetration will be permitted."

Her fate was inevitable. Perhaps it was best to have it over with. "When?"

"At bedtime he will share your nest, with or without your initial cooperation. Tomorrow the next in line shall attend you, then the next, until arbitration has ended. You will acquiesce immediately if you are wise. Remember what is at stake if you... misbehave."

Yes. They would publicly maim her mother... again.

Morgaine slumped back against the pillows, utterly defeated. "If Esin already has the greatest claim, then why draw out handing me over? Just give me to him and be done with it."

Sergeant Uriel gestured toward the fur scraps she

so pointedly refused. "Each pelt is a sampling of those who would contest his stake. As you can see, there are many soldiers to consider. Had you favored a scent from your nest, it would have altered the odds and ended arbitration more quickly. You have not done so."

There was a way to have a different outcome? Shooting up to her knees, Morgaine grabbed at the furs, holding a bunch up to her nose to sniff. "What if I favor one now?"

Crossing his arms over a barrel chest, Uriel scowled, entirely unamused. "It would be an illegitimate response. Had you recognized the scent of the most compatible male, you would not have scattered the fur away and tried your best to sleep uncovered despite modification to the room's temperature."

There was nothing to say, nothing that Alphas might listen to. Six days with these males and Morgaine knew ugly nursery rhymes were correct. Being born Omega was far worse than any evil.

Shaking his head at her stubborn silence, he warned, "You continually reject Alpha attention, are unaccustomed to adult urges—that will change quickly with this new curriculum." Reaching down, he took her hand and urged her from the bed. "Sexual release accelerates acceptance. You cannot know what it is Corporal Esin offers you, and so your fear is misplaced."

She knew what he offered. Every last muscle was still sore after what he'd done the day before.

The hollow feeling in her chest rattled with the deep vibrations the older man confidently projected. His purr might have been unwelcome, but the rumble was enough to allow her ribs to fully expand. Breath brought color to pale cheeks.

This was the submission they desired.

"Where I come from, being forced to have sex with strangers would see you executed by Alphas when they invaded to steal your crops and livestock."

Not a single flicker of compassion was to be found in Sergeant Uriel. Cold discipline, the true hardness of a tried and tested warrior—he was unmoved. "There is no Alpha on this ship who would cause you pain. All they want to offer is pleasure. Corporal Esin is no different. The decision is out of your inexperienced hands. As with all Omegas I have trained, you will thank me once you've grasped what a knot might bring you."

Even though she offered no resistance, Morgaine was dragged by her elbow to the table. Once seated, a plate was piled high.

"You will need your strength today. Eat."

The Omega swallowed the food Uriel had chosen for her without tasting a bite. Afterward, a bath was ordered, tonics given to be swallowed that he claimed would cheer her. For the first time ever, the sergeant stood over her as she soaked. He ordered she clean under her nails, lather her hair with soap, oil it with a slimy unguent left in a jar by the rim.

All the water drained.

"I did not command you to rise."

Half out of her seat, the soggy girl hesitated. She always hated this part, being wet and naked before an audience. But at least today the audience was not Corporal Esin.

Eyes on Uriel's boots, Morgaine rearranged herself and kept her eyes downcast. Wet hair lay plastered over her breasts. Legs together, hands in her lap to cover as much of her secret place as possible.

"Before we prepare for today, I have news for you."

Chin still tucked, she glanced up under her brows and waited for this *news*.

The Alpha looked pleased with himself, as if expectant to see her smile by what he would share. "Your genetics were run through our database to assure that none who offered for you were a blood relation."

Unsure how to answer, Morgaine lifted her brows.

"During this process, your patriarch was also discovered." Sergeant Uriel extended his arm, so she might obediently take his fingers. As she did, he added with a smile, "The Alpha in question was executed this morning."

"Executed?" Her mouth fell open, her foot missed the mark, and Morgaine's heel slipped on the tile.

Before she could do more than tangle her legs and bruise a shin, Sergeant Uriel caught her. He hauled her out and stood her far enough away from the ledge to prevent another accident. Steadying the girl, frowning, he said, "As I told you before, Alphas protect Beta settlements. Such a grievous breach of protocol had to be answered for. All are safe from him now. This should please you."

She had never thought of the male who'd fathered her as a real person. Even her mother had never spoken of it. Morgaine had only learned of such a thing from cruel neighborhood gossip. As a child she had questioned why her mother had been shunned, why she had no friends beyond her aunt.

It had been Hanna who had told Morgaine she was an Alpha's bastard when her boy had decided to play in their yard. She had said it as if letting her son play chase was the most magnanimous offering she might make as a neighbor.

Her mother had never complained, but there had been far-reaching consequences. No man in the settlement had asked for Elizabeta's hand, no matter her sweet smile or skill with needle and thread.

She was tainted in their eyes.

But they had one another. Their lives were quiet and happy, with no need of outside interference.

And though they had avoided her mother, the same neighbors had never been cruel to her. In harsh winters, no one went hungry. When her aunt's body had been found swinging from the rafters, many had come to offer solace.

As far as parentage, for all Morgaine knew, her mother had been a willing participant the day she was conceived.

And now her father was dead. Did he even know why? Had he too watched Esin rub between her legs?

Guilt, disgust, and shame left the Omega white as a sheet. Morgaine knew she had to answer, had to give Sergeant Uriel something or else a punishment might follow, so she muttered. "Alphas keep Betas safe."

Uriel was pleased, a smile in his eyes. "Well done, girl. You are learning."

She was learning. Every day she learned Alphas were closer to monsters than men. "What is my lesson today? Shall I sit in the chair and watch the screen?"

"No." Genuinely exultant, Uriel took her by the elbow and offered clothing. "Today we leave this room so that you can be introduced to those in the fleet with an interest in knowing you better."

10

───────

It took less than ten steps outside her room for Morgaine to discover that the Alphas' ship was *incredible*. In contradiction to her smooth-walled prison, the halls were etched, carved with jagged geometric shapes unlike anything she had seen in the settlement. Light seemed to emanate from the very metal—each glowing panel appearing warm to the touch. But the instant her fingers reached out to explore, her wrist was caught in a vise.

"Eyes forward, Morgaine. This is no place for an Omega to linger."

But why? After all those days tucked away, with the first inkling of excitement she'd felt since waking up in the sleeping pit, why could she not enjoy this? "I thought—"

"Don't think. Walk." Her guardian was stiff,

marching her forward with an air of menace he'd never displayed, even at his angriest in her room.

What happened to the reserved authority figure?

This aggressive warden—who held her wrist in a harsh pinch and yanked her to keep pace with his relentless gait—wasn't the aloof Sergeant Uriel he portrayed in private. Proof again that Alphas were never what they seemed.

Murderers, thieves, rapists… liars.

Trotting in an effort to keep up with the larger man, Morgaine knew better than to complain. After all, he was dragging her to meet potential suitors, and had already told her that when it was time for rest, Corporal Esin would be allowed to do more than use her hand to give himself pleasure.

No matter her feelings on the subject, Esin was going to rape her. Thrust over her flattened body like the Alpha she'd watched rutting the Omega on-screen.

Bunching shoulders, pinned wrists… slick or no, no matter what Sergeant Uriel claimed, Morgaine would never welcome such attention.

The man had ordered her mother's face to be branded. The same man treated her as his plaything.

Act in any way these Alphas might term as inso-lent? She would face *lessons*.

Mention her mother? Earn herself a caning and her mother a public whipping.

Walk too slow? Her arm would be yanked so hard her shoulder ached.

Stay silent? Be rebuked for not speaking.

Speak? Dark looks and castigation for failing to amaze.

They murdered a stranger because of one retort spoken in anger...

These Alphas didn't want Morgaine at all. They wanted the part of her Uriel referred to as a cunt. A cunt that dripped slick and was attached to a machine that made noises and did as it was told.

In the settlement, women did not leave their hair uncovered. They certainly didn't let men touch them without permission.

Rape was punishable by immediate execution.

Not here. Here Alphas did as they pleased.

Walking down those glittering corridors, Morgaine let that concept sink in. *Don't think. Walk.*

Don't complain. Obey.

You are no longer a person. You are property.

It did not even matter that their pace had left her flimsy garment loose, her left breast bouncing free of its covering. Not one of the males in the halls or galleries cared her modesty was gone or her hair flowed free and loose.

Don't live. Serve.

"Morgaine, pay attention. I'll not say it again." Pulling her to an abrupt stop, Sergeant Uriel turned on his charge and gave her a look that said now was not the time to misbehave.

Winded from the effort to keep up, feet aching from pounding against cold floors, Morgaine curled her toes and tried to catch her breath. "What?"

He did not release a frustrated sigh, but his glare alone made it seem Sergeant Uriel greatly desired to. Shoulders back, neck tense, he stood as if on display for the multitude of Alphas milling about the gallery.

It was *them*—the soldiers in their vermilion armor edging nearer—that had made him this way. Without thinking, immensely nervous to see so many eyes on her, Morgaine toed back a step. Uriel's tightening grip made retreat impossible. Staring at his face as he scanned the waiting crowd, the tense lines, the way his lip curled… the threatening growls offered to any who dared approach—she understood that she was prey in a room of circling predators. And only Uriel's snarls kept the beasts at bay.

There is no Alpha on this ship who would cause you pain. All they want to offer is pleasure.

These males didn't seem to have interest in her well-being, smirking, and glowering, and tasting the air.

"They are not permitted to touch you." Sergeant Uriel passed her into a glass enclosure, so small that any position other than standing would be almost impossible. "Present yourself for their inspection. Explain your situation and special handling."

She knew what he wanted her to say… what she was supposed to announce to all who showed interest, and frowned.

As if reading her closed expression and the taciturn intent of her thoughts, he amended, "Answer their questions. Show them your beauty and qualities. Behave."

Locking the entrance, Uriel stepped back and signaled that *introductions* could begin.

Surrounded in glass, males on all sides with nowhere to hide, hundreds, maybe even thousands, of Alphas were given their chance to approach and look upon her.

She was an item on display in the ship's main gallery, males stopping by to stare, to mark the tally with potential bids, and to handle an array of her used clothing. Clothing that Uriel had laid out after she'd been locked away. Even the filthy dress she was abducted in was fought over by the masses, lifted to the noses of strangers, each eyeing her as if she were to be devoured.

Before he'd left, Uriel reminded her to stand and be seen, to look at them, to answer their questions. Morgaine had not lasted ten minutes after his departure before she was crouched upon the floor, hiding her head in her knees.

She was discussed as if she wasn't there. "Why does it look unhappy?"

"According to her record, this Omega has yet to be knotted. It needs release." Someone banged his knuckles on the glass. "Omega, lift your head so we might see you."

She'd jumped at the taps, lifting red-rimmed eyes and setting them upon yet another stranger in vermilion armor. He looked like all the others, overly large, intimidating, and entitled. "My name is Morgaine. I have been ordered to tell you that I am feral. As of this morning I learned a feral designation necessitates I be separated from the regular female population for at least two years. I will require specific training." *Like a dog.* Her voice caught in her throat, Morgaine on the verge of tears. "It is suggested my future mate mount me multiple times a day, otherwise I might regress."

There were many males gathered, more stepping closer as she began to speak, only one of them asked, "Are you okay, Omega? I have never seen one of your kind cry."

She had been warned by Uriel that tears in front of potential mates were unacceptable, but she could not stop them from falling. The only thing she could do was lie in an effort to appease. "I am lonely. A mate will rectify this flaw in my character."

She couldn't do this. She couldn't face these men.

Forehead back to kneecaps, Morgaine breathed slow and deep, closed out the world around her, and tried her damnedest not to hear the males discussing her physical traits, her scent, the shade of her golden hair or the things they thought might cheer her— things that were all highly sexual in nature.

Where tears should have warned them off, it seemed it only made them desire her more.

A debate began on whether her first mating should be from behind so she would know the strength of her Alpha. Or, if she should be laid down in her nest and fucked from the front, where she might see and taste the male who would own her.

All agreed she should not be allowed to straddle an engorged Alpha cock—that was an honor she would have to earn.

More than one argued vehemently that her first time should be under the care of at least three males. That way they could keep her sticky with seed, stuff her full of cock, and break her in until exhaustion forced her to sleep. Three days of constant fucking would set her right... maybe more if she resisted.

The idea was atrocious.

Slumping down to the cold floor, Morgaine curled into a ball and squeezed her eyes shut until she saw spots.

She could not find it in her heart to care that the panel of her skirt would not cover her, that the men were shifting around her enclosure to glimpse whatever might be seen of her sex.

The males made a game of it—a series of growls projecting from one Alpha to the next to see who might get her pussy to twitch and leak a drop of slick first.

Not all calls were successful, but some did inspire the desired outcome. And there was nothing Morgaine could do to stop the inevitable, horrible, trickling response.

"Look at that pretty slit, all glossed and hungry. Do you want a cock, Omega? I can't wait to watch your first knotting."

Silently sobbing into her hands, mortified that something so personal would be broadcasted for the entire ship to view, Morgaine tried her damnedest to shut them out. She'd hated what made her Omega— her body's shameful betrayal, loathed how little control she had when the bone shaking rumbles were made.

Mostly, she hated the males who cheered, shouting encouragement for her to open her thighs and give them an even closer look.

Leaning up on an elbow, she let them see her tearmarked cheeks and tried to communicate that she was more than a hole they all could fuck. "I have great skill in dying cloth. I can make rare greens and purples from ingredients local to our forest in shades so vibrant they were highly sought after by my neighbors." She didn't know who she was pleading with, the males too caught up in their game to listen, but Morgaine muttered on all the same. "I know the traditional dances to flute music and sew well. At harvest, I am useful in the fields. I had friends…"

Silence slowly broke up the noise, a sense of quiet amidst the sound of shuffling feet eerie. Whatever had ended the raucous tableau, she didn't know. She didn't care. She just hoped they were listening.

They were not. Sergeant Uriel had returned into their midst, growling with heavy disapproval at the raucousness of the crowd and the pathetic figure she displayed. "Stand up, Omega. Stand now and keep your eyes downcast." His low bark harsher than she'd yet heard. "I will not have you be seen this way."

Pressing her palm to the floor, she shifted to her knees, looking over her shoulder to see an older male had come to view her shame. His rank had to be high if the glittering marks on his armor were any indication. He did not at all look pleased.

Climbing to her feet, she did exactly as she was told, kept her eyes downcast, and shoulders straight.

"Commandant, this is Morgaine of the Ivex Colony on the fourth continent of Nauu. She was harvested from one of our more resourceful settlements." Sergeant Uriel stood at stiff attention, listing her attributes as if selling a horse. "Her eyes are blue, hair golden, long in the fashion of their females. She speaks only the common language and has been educated by farmers. A simple girl, with simple skills, but great beauty."

Mortified to be spoken of as if lacking, Morgaine's cheeks went red, but she kept her lips sealed.

"Why was it lying on the floor?"

Sergeant Uriel did not soften his assessment in the slightest. "This one is feral, Commandant. She is indolent and argumentative. As such, her handling has been strict and her education requirements adjusted to diminish her flaws. She needs more training than most."

The commandant shook his head, lips thinned. "I have heard enough of this case, and frankly, I'm tired of the petitions. Her presence on my ship has been a distraction to the ranks, and to come here and find her exposed, enticing my soldiers to quicken her pleasure, it cannot be tolerated. Look at her thighs… they are dripping with slick. This sort of lewd behavior is only tolerable in the pleasure quarters for those who've earned the right to be entertained by an Omega, not in the main gallery by any passing male."

"She is a virgin, sir. Her body is preparing for penetration. We also suspect she is on the verge of her first estrous."

It was intolerable, and Morgaine could not bite her

tongue. "I did not ask them to growl at me, nor did I like it. Don't think I'm doing this on purpose!"

"Silence!" The commandant's roar shook her, causing Morgaine to back away.

Sergeant Uriel was equally incensed. "Do not speak again, Morgaine."

Measuring the shrinking Omega, bushy brows drawn low over unforgiving eyes, the commandant decided her fate. "If you don't want it to sit, then sitting shall be made painful. Three strikes with a cane across her buttocks. Two across the shoulders. Tomorrow we shall see how straight she stands and how seriously she takes this honor. If I find her lying down again, the punishment will be doubled. Omegas must know their place."

PUNISHMENT WAS SERVED IMMEDIATELY. Amidst the grumbled disappointment of the males who had yet to push their way to the front of the crowd, Morgaine was pulled from her glass cage. Pulled rather roughly.

Marched back through the halls, dragged when she couldn't keep up, past gawking strangers. When they found her door, she watched Sergeant Uriel press his hand to the wall and it opened at once.

Thrust inside, she found Corporal Esin, smiling, the room decorated with flickering lights and smelling of a savory meal. He took one look at Uriel's stormy countenance and lost all traces of joy.

"She is to be caned."

Already reaching to strip off his tunic, Esin declared, "I'll bear her punishment. As many strikes as you see fit, sir."

"You will not." The door closed at his back, the smooth wall seamless, before Uriel released her aching arm. "Five strikes were ordered by the commandant as a necessary reminder of what she is and who she owes her fealty to. For her disrespect to your leadership, I am adding another strike."

"Sir." Crestfallen, Esin gave her a look that set her skin bumping in fear. "Six strikes… she's so small."

"You may brace her and offer comfort as it's done."

And it was done at once. A dumbfounded Morgaine was dragged into her sleeping pit and shoved down to sprawl on her belly. Between them they moved her where they would, the girl too shell-shocked to grasp what was coming.

Esin held her forearms. Pulling them away from her body and planting them into the floor with his weight. Hair gathered and moved away from her back, clothing tugged aside before she could complain… she didn't even know where Sergeant Uriel had procured the cane.

A shrill whistle and searing fire tore a line across

the naked cheeks of her ass. It happened so quickly, with no break between strikes, that by the third she was sobbing and fighting to get away.

All the while, Esin whispered that if she remained still, the bite of the cane would cause less damage. *He pled with her*.

The fourth caught her across the shoulders, the hardest strike yet, landing on a girl so beyond the ability to cope that she shrilled out a cry for help from the very man holding her down. By the fifth she was begging for mercy, saying anything she thought they might want to hear to get the pain to stop.

The sixth fell and she was certain she was going to die.

Breaking the cane over his knee, Sergeant Uriel threw it across the room, shattering a pitcher on the table. "May that sting remind you that though we do not enjoy doling out punishment on our females, we will!"

He stormed out, leaving the stink of Alpha anger and something even more terrifying— *compunction* —in the air. The burden of remorse had not held back his rage; even under its sting Sergeant Uriel had still beaten her into perfect submission

…and he'd abandoned her to Esin's care.

Slumped over the pillows, the flesh of her back and buttocks seared as if from open flame, Morgaine put up no fight when the corporal circled to her back. No resistance was offered when he pet unmarked skin.

It was time to get it over with and accept that she'd been cast into hell.

This male had the right to enter her now. And then tomorrow another. And then another. And another.

The threat that had been hanging over her head would be carried out while she was in too much pain to do a damn thing.

Instead, he blew cool breath over the marks, speaking softly. "There is no blood. He was surprisingly delicate. The sergeant could have struck you hard enough to split skin and leave scars."

Hating the world, Morgaine sobbed. "My only value here is in my beauty…"

Esin did not answer her, blowing again as if a soft puff of air might soothe her. "As this was a punishment, I am forbidden to heal you. All I can offer is ice for the pain."

And he did, cautious in how he cooled the fire of each mark. While he tended to her, he spoke of his disappointment, of how he had thought to impress her upon her return. "I spent a great deal on the best foods available on this ship. There is even a bottle of Hessmirn wine I've been saving just for you. For my beloved mate."

Morgaine didn't argue with the creature sliding ice

over scalding fires. She only nodded in hopes of appeasing him.

"When you've calmed down, I'll make you a plate. Don't move a muscle, just rest, sweet renegade."

And thus the night progressed. Esin was with her until she slept, iced her wounds when she whimpered. Offered water, wine, food, anything he thought she might require.

Not once did he initiate mating. It would have been impossible to do without hurting her more.

For that, Morgaine was almost grateful.

11

The commandant's punishment produced the desired effects. Morgaine could not sit, nor could she comfortably lean against the glass cage she was once again locked inside. On display for the second time in as many days, she stood still as stone in the center of the enclosure exactly as they wanted her to.

When she was asked a question, she answered it. When foreign males picked up the clothing outside her cage to sniff, she pretended she didn't see their reaction or the way many would reach down and adjust their growing erections.

"What is your name?"

"Morgaine."

"Show me your breasts, Morgaine."

Staring over their heads, the panels of her garment were pulled apart, taut nipples catching the fabric until fleshy orbs bounced free.

Unlike the day before, she didn't wallow. In fact, she did not allow herself to feel anything. Almost robotic, she went through the motions, kept her eyes off them, and even forced smiles when told to—though her face always returned to neutral once she'd performed to their liking.

"Have you been trained in pleasuring an Alpha?"

"No. I am feral and have never been mounted. I have only seen matings via the screen in my room. The details were obscured."

Alpha males were cycling through the data log at the base of her enclosure, one of them commenting aloud. "Corporal Esin holds the greatest stake. Do you see that, Regis? He won't be of rank to take a mate for at least two years. Should his suit win, she will be made available for use in the pleasure quarters until he can legally claim her."

Sergeant Uriel had never once mentioned such a thing to her.

Apathy dropped away, as did Morgaine's stomach. "What?"

The males did not answer her, their conversation continuing between them. "The corporal will grow rich with her rental, and we can apply to share her company together. Look here, she has been cleared to service up to five males at a time… ten while in estrous. By the time she is under his pair-bond, he'll have rank, status, money, and a well-trained Omega eager to please him. It's brilliant, really."

The soldier's friend chuckled. "No wonder his case is so strongly petitioned. He must have financial backers impatient to take a cut of the profit."

Any softness Morgaine might have felt after Esin's tender care the previous night evaporated. She took a step toward the glass, and tapped her knuckles against the panel to get the males' attention. "Great Alpha soldiers, can you please clarify?"

They ignored her, scrolling down the file and whistling at what they found.

Desperate for an explanation, she looked around, trying to make eye contact with any male. It was not her eyes they were staring at: breast, thigh, the width of her hips and taper of her waist. Her eyes were inconsequential.

She, Morgaine, was invisible. Only her body mattered.

Looking down at her hands, at her manicured nails, the temptation to set them to her flesh and tear grew overwhelming. If she could just make herself ugly, they might leave her alone.

…or they would heal her and chain her hands.

Frantically working the simple tie of her dress, she pulled the cloth away so all gathered might see her bared. "I want a mate, any mate. I do not wish to work in the pleasure quarters. Who can pay more than Esin? What do I have to do to please you?"

Finally, she had their attention. The male reading her file shook his head. "He was clever in structuring his bid. The sum here is great, more than I can afford. But, when it is my turn to visit you, I will pay the fee and treat you well."

Her fanatic pitch grew, Morgaine's palms banging loudly against the glass. "Is there anyone else who can pay more?"

Not one of them offered for her, even if several looked as if they wanted her more than anything in the world.

No wonder so many had been collecting outside her containment. No wonder they were interested in reading the file and scenting her clothing. Each of them would have a chance to know her intimately… for a fee.

For two whole years…

She had one chance to change her fate, throwing back her shoulders to announce, "I am feral, but I would be a good mate. I am industrious and hard-working."

Someone behind her cracked a joke. "The marks across your ass would say differently."

Breathless, flustered, Morgaine continued. "Never once was I punished in my settlement. I am loyal and loving. Do not Alphas want to be loved by an Omega? I… I know how to collect and store rare herbs. I can weave baskets, sew clothing. Three of my neighbors' houses I helped build. I bred goats that made fine milk and cheese."

They were starting to laugh at her ridiculous list of attributes, not one skill listed useful in their society.

Altering tactics, she said, "I can be the perfect servant. Is that what you want?"

"And you will be… in the pleasure quarters."

Speechless, completely lost, Morgaine backed away. Glassy eyes went to the floor, to where her dress lay in a heap. Bending down to take it set the wounds on her back to burning at the stretch of skin. But she could not bear to remain naked and begging. Not before these horrible *things*.

She'd rather bear the pain of the cane over and over than submit to so many for so little. "Any who come to me in the pleasure quarters I will bite."

That was the wrong thing to say, for immediately several pushed closer.

"I will scratch you, make you bleed."

The bright-eyed male nearest the front licked his lips.

Locking eyes with him, she hissed, "I will hate

you and cry the whole time. You and all Alphas disgust me."

"Silence, feral, before you earn yourself more punishment than you can handle."

One thing Morgaine was good at on this ship was digging her own grave. It seemed the perfect time to pick up the shovel. "I would rather be burned at the stake in front of everyone I loved, than feel the touch of a single one of you."

Thoughts a riot of ugly things and evil outcomes, she became stone, ignoring their growled responses to her rudeness, refusing to answer questions. They grew bored of her, and over the hours, began to scatter.

Morgaine had done her reputation harm, but she did not care.

There was nothing in the world to care about.

Oblivious to her heart-pounding anxiety, Alphas ceased strolling, moving aside in automatic formation. They left her cage abandoned for the first time since she'd been locked inside that morning, and gave her a view of the massive gallery.

A vast room that, aside from the shuffle of footsteps, was a suddenly, eerily silent place.

Bracing, sure the commandant was coming to cast an unfavorable judgment upon her, Morgaine swallowed and took a deep breath.

Maybe they'd cut out her tongue, just as these men had done to her aunt years ago.

Maybe they would see her raped at last.

From the glitter of armor on the opposite end of the room, he had arrived, as had several high-ranked Alphas at his back. Stiffening her shoulders, she prepared to look her tormenter in the eye as he decided her next punishment.

But his attention was not on her. Instead he stood at the front of his men… waiting.

Squinting to see, Morgaine could hardly make out what they were doing across the vast space. Columns supporting the room's high ceiling made spying difficult, as did the bright backlight of glowing metal at their backs, but something of great consequence made the air buzz with inevitability.

Every soldier in attendance had stepped into formation, as if banking a parade. All eyes cast toward the front of the room.

A secondary group entered. Alphas by the size of them, but not dressed in the vivid vermilion armor of the thousands waiting in their regimented lines.

Nor were these males trimmed and barbered. Long hair, some sported beards… and skin.

Bare chests, corded arms, some wore little more than strips of tanned leather around their hips.

Whoever the group was, they didn't look a thing like any Alpha who had ever invaded her settlement. Their wild state, the fact they paraded before armored soldiers with no care for their menace made her nervous.

Even from a distance, she could sense their contempt for all they saw.

Not a word could be made out, but the commandant bowed, as did all those glittering with rank at his back. The new males did not return the gesture.

If the older Alpha was insulted by the lack of respect, he didn't show it. He gestured for what must have been their leader to join him.

For reasons unknown, she broke out in a cold sweat, knowing that if they crossed the length of the gallery, they would walk past her.

These Alphas, the savagely dressed dark-haired behemoths, needed to stay far, far away.

No soul in the room was looking at her. She had been forgotten. But trapped in glass with nowhere to go, she felt the most exposed of her life.

The reason was those in formation near her. Yes, they were riveted on the scene, but not one of them looked gratified. In fact, the taste of air she had beyond the glass was animosity, bitterness... even a hint of fear.

Who were these men?

Formalities aside, these guests... if they *were* guests... were not welcome. Nor could they have been expected. They looked like raiders; scoffed and sneered at all they saw, brushing off the formality staged before them as the two groups converged.

Commandant and dark-haired savage leader both turned, walking down the center path that would lead past where she'd been caged. There was no conversation between them. That would require the practically naked male beside the old man to reply to anything that was being said.

It seemed he pointedly ignored the high-ranked escort, staring straight ahead and walking with purpose. Upon their approach, Morgaine found these men to be even stranger. Her initial assessment was right; they wore their hair almost as long as she wore hers. On many, scars were prominently displayed: slashes across bared chests, shiny star-shaped splatters of mended skin.

Though she'd never seen a wound of that sort healed, she had seen many of her neighbors die from blaster fire. She'd seen the way the skin around the wound flashed out like a bursting flower.

Warriors?

Was this some ritual? Is that why so much skin was exposed?

Were these elite soldiers?

Their features didn't look like the other men. Cheekbones higher, brows harsh.

Foreign.

They looked rough, these men, rougher than their

shined, vermilion armored counterparts. In comparison, they looked monstrous.

Sharp pain jarred her, Morgaine instinctively backing away until her welted and bruised back hit the glass. Her hiss went ignored, for the men were still too far down the gallery to hear her and those near seemed to have forgotten she existed.

The commandant was in conversation with a scowling, square-jawed male at the front of the cavalcade. Like the others, this one wore a weapon at his hip. It did not look like the blasters or knives of the Alphas Morgaine knew. In fact, she would not have thought it a weapon at all except that the commandant looked to it multiple times. When he did so, it was with the same disgust he had projected upon her the day before.

Under that disgust was concern.

It made Morgaine more nervous to see a man as hard and mean as he display veiled hesitation.

They were near enough now she could hear them speaking, but only one language Morgaine understood. With a low timbre and a scratchy grumble, the *guest* gave throaty responses an unseen male at his back translated.

This was a true foreigner.

Settlers told stories about alien peoples, about harsh cruelties that drove her kind to these new worlds. In the tales, the men described were just as coarse as those marching closer.

And closer, and closer.

Close enough now that several in his party had seen her, seen how she pulled her hair over her shoulders as if to hide behind it… how she only looked at them from the corner of her eye.

They stared as if confused by such a sight, grumbling between themselves in their rough language.

Worried she'd offended, that she had earned more than just another beating, Morgaine glanced to their leader and found him stopped dead in his tracks.

He was staring right at her, speaking quickly in a collection of growls and hisses.

Whatever the translation was, she couldn't hear it over the beating of her heart in her ears.

The ferocity she'd leveled at the Alphas earlier had dried up, just like her mouth. It might as well have been full of sand.

Their eyes met.

The weighted stare of a demon held her in terrified thrall.

Morgaine forgot to breathe, to blink.

The foreign monster put a hand to the commandant's chest when he tried to step between them and shoved him back. The old man sprawled, and heavy footfalls beat the ground, dark hair flying out behind the snarling Alpha as he charged her cage.

Others flew after him, trailing behind the male

running full speed toward her cage. He reached the glass, gathered the dress she'd worn the day before, the one that had been left out to be pawed and sniffed by strangers. He held it to his nose, roared, and brought both fists to pound the clear barricade between them.

As he beat the glass, as cracks formed and the whole cage trembled, Morgaine screamed.

She screamed and screamed, backing away, curling up as if to hide no matter the welts or the pain.

If she could have made herself invisible, if she could have willed her soul away, she would have. Because the devil was roaring for it, and the cracks in the glass were growing.

Men fell upon him, men in vermilion armor and men in leather alike. It took an entire swarm to pull the bellowing beast away, even more to quell the growing rumble between the two groups. She saw him dragged from the room, saw the veins and muscles standing up in his neck, his snapping teeth, and the way his eyes were locked only on her.

What he shouted in his ugly tongue, whether they were curses or threats, Morgaine did not know. She'd pressed her hands over her ears, still screaming even as Sergeant Uriel entered to gather her up.

The mangled scents of the room hit her, the stink of furious musk, a cacophony of men, of sweat, of agitation, of fear... of hunger.

The instant she felt hands on her, she fought, biting and scratching just as she'd threatened the others. But one Alpha was much stronger than one traumatized Omega. The male ignored her thrashing, and rushed her away in the opposite direction.

12

It was the nest she dove for the instant Morgaine was set free. The hated scraps of fur were burrowed under, Morgaine instinctively seeking cover no matter the orders any might snap or punishments that might be ordained.

No one tried to pull her out from where she hid, not even Sergeant Uriel barked an order. His hands were full dealing with several Alphas who'd entered the chamber behind them. Their voices could be heard arguing amongst themselves, meaning muffled by the hands she'd pressed over her ears.

They left her alone.

Light weight even came to land over where she trembled, as if blankets had been draped to cover where a foot or leg were exposed by inadequate furs.

In all her time in this horrible new place, with all

the fear and uncertainty she'd endured over her *instruction*, never in her life had she been more terrified than in those heart-stopping moments watching the cracks grow in the glass.

She imagined she could still hear him, hear him shouting and the pounding of his fists as he roared and went mad.

"Corporal Esin! Do not approach the nest or touch her!" Sergeant Uriel boomed so all might hear. "That goes for all of you. The Omega is off limits."

An unfamiliar voice spoke up. "Sir, she was supposed to be *mine* tonight."

Real anger came from the sergeant. "Did I stutter?"

"You cannot leave her unattended in this state. I have a legal right to calm her."

She didn't know who Uriel spoke to, but Morgaine heard the command clearly. "Remove him from the room."

The sounds of a struggle were short-lived. When the door closed, it grew quiet enough she heard the footsteps approaching where she'd burrowed.

"Morgaine, you are completely safe in here. The Omari cannot reach you. Come out of there so that I may see that you are unhurt."

Nothing was going to move her, no amount of Alpha purrs, no threats. They would have to pull her kicking and screaming from the covers.

"Under these circumstances it would be appropriate to offer sedation. Medic, hand over the dram."

In a flurry, the covering over her leg was whipped back. Before she could kick, a prick nicked her skin, and the scream prepared in her throat died on a sigh.

Pleasurable feeling washed over her, a mirror of that same warm safety she'd woken from that first morning. Drugs battled against her adrenaline, and between them, a drifting middle ground was found.

"She may not be able to sit up on her own with such a high dose." The medic spoke, but it was Uriel she found carefully lifting away the layers she hid under.

When she saw the bleeding set of gashes across his cheek, Morgaine knew she had put them there. Just as she'd bit his hand to the point skin had broken. Even now blood stained her lips and flavored her tongue.

Half drunk, Morgaine took in the entirety of him and muttered, "You hit me with a stick. I'd rather be a lowly, feral Omega than an Alpha dog any day."

Sergeant Uriel didn't blink. He reached down, pulling her up to lean against the cushions despite her welts. "Her inhibition response is muted by the dram. Any slurs made now are off the record and forgiven."

In that case, she was going to lay it all out. "And you"—sluggish eyes traveled to where Esin stood by —"you were going to whore me out for profit to the panting vermin outside my glass cage. I didn't think it was possible to hate someone as much as I hate you. I was wrong. I *haaaate* you."

He seemed genuinely forlorn to hear her slander and equally shocked by her obvious knowledge of what might be. "You misunderstand, renegade. I do not possess the rank to claim a mate yet. But with hard work, I could initiate a pair-bond in less than two years. What is a lifetime of joy to a few moments of disappointment? Do you think I rejoice in knowing other men will relish your time, that you will delight in their bodies during the hours I'm required by law to share you? I do not. It's the only way we can be together as we are meant to be."

It was not like her to use gross language, but, slurring, Morgaine swore, "I'd rather fuck every last disgusting Alpha on this ship than have you so much as look at me."

Three snaps of calloused fingers came before her blurring vision. "That's enough, Morgaine. Focus here." Uriel kneeled so they were at eye level. "Are you hurt?"

Nodding, tears began to fall. "Everything you do here hurts."

Despite knowing better, Morgaine crumpled, begging over and over for her mother.

"There will be no getting through to her in this

state. Hand me another dose. She will be examined after she falls asleep."

This time the prick came to her shoulder, and shortly after, she lay limp as a fresh corpse.

A METALLIC TASTE sat heavy on her tongue, arms and legs weighted by the remnants of waning sedatives. She had yet to move or open her eyes, prone on her belly, soft coverings on her back. There were voices in the room—no longer by the door as they had been before, but near the area where the room's table always lay laden with food.

"How many of his men do you think their Heidron has killed trying to break out?"

The Alphas were laughing, one offering up, "At least he does our work for us. Omari scum coming here with no warning… fresh treaty or no, we do not bow to their whims."

It didn't matter what the men at her table boasted or claimed. She herself had seen the commandant bow to the foreigners.

"It is no laughing matter." Uriel cut off the revelry. "I advise you each to count the friends, brothers, and children you lost in the war. Hold on to that number and keep your silence before I make you silent. To imagine there will be no far-stretching repercussion from what took place in the gallery displays our arrogant blindness the Omari exploited in the first place. *We surrendered to them.* Remember that."

Petulant, Esin disagreed. "Had our colonies not been threatened, sir, the outcome would have gone the other way. They do not value Beta life as we do, just as they are known to rape and mutilate their Omegas. They're animals. He cannot be allowed to have her. She'll die."

"You are not pair-bonded to the girl, and unless she enters estrous in the next hour, you have no means to seal a claim. Their warships have already begun to appear around our fleet. The Heidron is going to demand she be handed over once his rut subsides, or he will take her by force. Our commandant will have no choice. He will not risk rekindling a bloody war for one feral Omega."

So, they were going to hand her over to that raving creature from the pit. Considering their lies thus far of promised safety and love, Morgaine felt no surprise at such news.

Whatever she had done to offend that rabid male, she knew he'd kill her, and then at least it would be over. Considering how fiercely he'd battered the glass, her death would most likely be quick.

It was for the best.

The pleasure chambers would have shredded away

her honor. Being mated to Esin would have been a lifetime of misery.

Groaning, she fought the covers and sat up. Rubbing away the crust from her eyes, she heard the males push back their chairs and stand.

Before one of them might give her a command or ask any pointed questions, she mumbled, "My bladder is full."

Uriel ordered the men away, but he did not leave her to her own devices. In fact, he watched her like a hawk, which made relieving herself difficult. When the act was finished, he ordered her to bathe, ordered her to dress herself, and ordered her to eat.

She went through the motions, still numb, and unsure if it was a lingering effect of the drug or if her spirit had simply flown away.

As if reading her thoughts, Sergeant Uriel sighed. "I imagine it won't be much longer now."

He was correct.

The commandant himself entered, a small army waiting in the hall when that shining wall opened up wide. "Come, Omega, you are to go to the Omari Heidron now. May he be merciful."

Lips stained berry red from the flesh of the fruit she'd forced down, Morgaine stood. Damp hair curling past her waist, life stolen away, she marched where she was bidden.

Though the remnants of sedation still tickled her veins, fear found a way to bloom with each step.

The *thing* they were giving her to, she remembered the wild look in his eyes. That Alpha was the stuff of nightmares: scarred, barbaric, and brimming with menace.

His people were powerful enough to have subjugated the Alpha soldiers and entered their ship.

Esin claimed they raped and mutilated Omegas.

She was going to die horribly.

And so continued her slow march, one where not even Uriel touched her to drag her onward. Heart thudding behind her ribs, her cadence wavered, and she was unsure if she could walk farther… but it was already too late.

Morgaine's eyes never left the ground, but she knew those foreign Alphas were just ahead. She could smell their sweat, the soft aroma of leather, hear their grumbled murmurs.

Gruff, the commandant broke the lingering silence. "You are aware that this Omega is flawed? Your men briefed you on her shortcomings?"

Translation began at once, flowing, familiar speech turning guttural.

The beast replied, his voice a rasp of grit and dirt.

Moments later, the translator shared the menacing male's words. Words that were only for her. "I have brought you a gift, gentle girl. Will you not look at me so I might give it to you?"

Her lip was shaking, so she sucked it into her mouth and bit down. Nails sharp against her palms, the pain familiar, Morgaine made herself obey. Inch by inch her chin went up, eyes following until she saw what was held out before her.

It was a mangy fur still in the shape of whatever brown animal it had been torn from, large enough to dwarf her if unraveled fully, and ugly as sin.

"I…"

The brute came toward her, Uriel pressing his hands to her spine to prevent her immediate retreat. With a swish, the skin was draped over her shoulders, covering her near nudity and offering warmth.

He spoke again, translation offered immediately. "I didn't have anything finer prepared, but I could not have you cold and uncovered to be gawked at by these cowards."

It was an odd gesture considering the Alphas she knew. They had never once cared if she was cold in their swath of fabric, and they certainly didn't want her body covered from sight. Calling them cowards, though, seemed like an unwise choice.

The monstrous male began purring loudly, his hands coming to rest on her shoulders. There he kneaded tense muscle, putting his nose to her hair for a deep sniff.

Under the influence of that noise, of his nearness, her knees almost gave out. Instead they knocked together, and she drew in a shuddering breath.

She'd yet to look up to his face, eyes trained on a long scar across his chest, mouth dry, and fingers clutching at the draping fur as if it might shield her, Morgaine endured.

The careful fingers at her shoulders closed tighter, pulling her toward that naked, scarred chest as the male spoke to those who brought her. "This female is ripe."

The commandant answered, short and cold. "She's nearing her first estrous. Do not account for her age. As I said, she is flawed."

Purr increasing in volume, his words soft despite the rasp and ugliness of his language, the foreigner spoke and the translator supplied, "If you use that word again to describe my *kor'yr*, I will rip out your throat, castrate your children, and see that your mate is defiled."

She breathed out, tried to pull away, but her resistance went unheeded. He cupped the back of her head, pressing her cheek to his heart, just as his other arm clamped around her waist.

Locked tight to a stranger's body, wrapped in the coarse skin of an unknown animal, frightened, Morgaine whimpered.

The fingers at her skull drew soft circles even as he held her tighter.

Purr intensifying, engulfing and abundant, it drowned out all else. She could feel it in each cell and hear it in a way that was too intimate to ignore. His offering was in her and around her, just as an enticing scent filled her lungs with each breath.

They had doused him in something that smelled appealing, a lie to cover his brutality. But like the purr, it did its work. Muscles loosened, her heart rate normalized, and Morgaine closed her eyes to it all.

"That's it, princess. Fear does not suit you." Warm fingers began to burrow deeper against her scalp, working their way down her neck and back up again until she let out an easy breath. "Come, I will show you what it means to be the kor'yr of Heidron Simin Gralloch."

13

The transport ship shook under their feet, Morgaine gawking at the view from the porthole. Outside that window a whole planet glowed, hundreds of other ships hovering above the atmosphere around it.

Her home world, there, so close all along.

It looked so big and so small, the swirled green-blue mass indescribable. Beauty like that was enough to keep her head turned away from the frightening male who held her close, twisting the length of her golden hair in his fist like a leash.

He wanted her attention, broadcasting it with a soft tug at her roots.

They rape and mutilate their Omegas.

Esin's soft spoken warning to Uriel had done its

work, just as the savage's purr was waging war against her fear.

When she still refused to look away from the view, battle roughened fingers tripped over the front of her throat, a large thumb pushing her jaw until Morgaine was forced to stare upward. His face sat in her view, inches from hers, but still she kept her gaze diverted. The male touched her lower lip with his thumb, pulling it to the side in a sweep, even as a low noise came from his throat.

Her eyes were on home.

The fingers on her neck trilled, the grip on her hair tightened. She wasn't going to get another warning. Little stings against her scalp made her bow back further, to grip his forearm so she would not lose her balance.

Rape and mutilate.

Those two things this male would do to her. What was the point in refusing to meet his gaze?

A shallow breath, and she obeyed.

His eyes weren't blue like hers or particularly pretty. They were too murky to be named a single color. One of them was ringed in an ugly bruise. Below, cheekbones were defined but not sharp, hollow cheeks, and a strong jaw.

Extreme masculinity with nothing soft or gentle.

Not even his lips could be called soft, though they

ever so slightly curled up at the corners the instant her attention was on them.

He said something to her, a series of low-pitched warbles.

Not one of the other males on this ship offered a translation, though she glanced around in hope for an explanation.

Her distraction was exploited. The Heidron put his mouth on hers.

The attack had been well-coordinated. Her head hit his bicep, his fingers pinching her jaw open so he could steal a taste. Female squeal squelched by a lapping tongue in her mouth, Morgaine found he held her immobile, that he possessed total control.

With his fingers pinching her cheeks, she could not even bite.

The male took his time exploring her taste, the edges of her teeth, swallowing down her nervous pants, careless that others openly watched.

Skin prickling from a creeping flush, Morgaine sagged and let him do what he wished. Nips on her lips kept them parted, an undulating tongue teased. It wasn't like the teeth shattering kisses Esin had forced on her mouth.

This male conquered with cleverness, not violence. And though he ran his hand carefully over her throat and collarbones, he didn't paw.

But he would.

Unsolicited Alpha attention continued the entire flight from ship to ship, endured by a confused woman who did not understand why his fingers were so careful, or why he didn't grunt at her like Esin did when she failed to adequately return the kiss.

It seemed he didn't mind her lack of participation. In fact, the more still she grew, the more excited the Alpha became. The smell of musk dripped from his pores; it was rubbed on her, unavoidable like that tongue playing between her teeth.

When the ship docked and the door opened, he set her free, only to gather her up against his chest before she might take so much as a step. The others were left behind as he marched forward to the riotous sound of cheering men.

Holding her tightly to him, he gave a single triumphant shout in return. When she startled, when fear bloomed all the brighter, his march through the hangar became a rushed affair.

Corridor, corridor, corridor, left, too many turns to count, a beep and a slick slide of a door.

Through the mad race, he had his paws on her anywhere he might reach without dropping her, his tongue on her skin like a slavering dog. The fur, her slim protection, was yanked away. A hand came to her chest, Morgaine pushed back until she fell into weightlessness.

Pillows cushioned impact, but not the sting against

raised welts and aching bruises. And then the beast was over her, grinning, speaking guttural nonsense she could not understand, even as he tore at her clothes.

This she expected. This is how they all were.

The instant he had her naked, the Alpha stilled. Arms locked, muscles protruding, he panted and stared. Pink nipples, he licked his lips to see them. Her belly, flat and velvety, brought to his face a lecherous grin.

Legs caught outside his hips, Morgaine was fully exposed when that hungry gaze slid lower. Her slit shined with dampness, sweet slick smeared across her inner thighs... the same damn fluid that had plagued her body since she'd been taken from her cottage.

She tried to cover herself when a trickle leaked from her slit to drip between her cheeks. "I don't know how to make it stop."

With a grunt, both her hands were batted aside, wrists caught and pinned. He even shifted his knees to spread her further, to see the little, twitching mouth of her cunt waiting behind soft lower lips.

Pink, pretty, contracting in tight pulses at such direct attention.

Noises beyond the purr were coming from the barbarian, low threatening growls that turned her body against her fear.

On his lowest rumble, a rush of fluid spurted from

her cunt, leaving Morgaine shocked, embarrassed, and trying to squirm away.

The more she moved, the more the grinning male countered.

He grumbled more words at her, lowering his head as he did so. He chased until her hips were caught and hooked over his shoulders. A broad tongue swept up as much of her slick in a single lick as it could, gathered it in his mouth to be savored.

He closed his eyes, offered a low, ravenous moan, and swallowed.

This had never been displayed on the wall during lessons. What he was doing was unseemly, Morgaine squealing when his mouth descended for another taste.

The other part of the Alpha was supposed to be jammed inside of her, not the tongue that had gone right back to licking her slit. It prodded her hole, played with the fleshly wet lips, worst of all, flicked at a part of her that made her gasp and choke on air.

No Sergeant Uriel was going to come into the room and tell the male to stop. Her pleas were nothing to him. In fact, they were not even making sense to her own ears.

On and on the brute feasted, Morgaine's eyes rolling back in her head.

There was a sense of powerlessness that stole the air from the room, that made her pant and wriggle—

that even spread her thighs as if she wanted more. Buzzing skin, a great swirling crest of feeling…

And then she cried out, a burst of heat in her belly stealing all sense. Lava flowed through her veins, twisted her guts, and burned all the hotter as the male flicked the tip of his tongue even faster over that nub of sensation.

Her wrist was set free, her hand going to his forehead to push him away… but it was too late. Fingers pointed like a javelin, he pushed them knuckle deep into her sopping, twitching cunt.

Her inner muscles grabbed at those digits, fighting to draw them deeper, to clamp down around them while the rest of her spasmed uncontrollably.

It felt as if it would never end, the evil he was working on her body. Worse, it felt so good she could not stop the way she begged for more and rolled her hips against his wriggling fingers.

When the tide of pleasure slowly abated, she was boneless, tender and swollen between her legs, and caught lying back with a stranger's fist partway in her body. Smiling down at her, he pulled it out slowly, carefully, despite her inner muscles trying their best to hold on tight.

He rubbed that hand, slippery with her fluids across his bare chest, leaving a mark of shine.

Next his fingers went to his belt, Morgaine unsure what to do.

She was not even sure of who she was in that moment.

Leather parted, the Alpha fisting a hard cock, stroking it as he stared down at her.

The crown was swollen, dripping beads of pearly fluid. The shaft was pulsating in a continuous throb, many times thicker than the Beta males' she'd seen on the screen. At the base of it, a bulbous knot already hinted at what was sure to be far more than she could handle.

He was going to force that monstrosity in her, just as the Alpha had done on the screen.

Watching her face, the male continued to stroke that huge organ, speaking lowly in a rhythm of guttural consonants and growls. The things he said, she was certain translation was not desired. They were filthy things, disgusting things, things that would shame her more than he already had.

Why else would he look at her that way?

With one hand he took her shoulder and urged her to turn over. There was no fight, her body still reeling from sparks of raw feeling and her spirit trapped by his purr. On her knees, bracing her hands against the edge of his sunken bed, Morgaine let him draw her hips up high, and closed her eyes tight.

She felt him sweep her hair from her back and… and then she felt nothing.

He was not touching her, though he still knelt

between her spread thighs. The heat of his body was certain, but he did not move.

Bracing for pain, Morgaine's every muscle went tight. Still he did not penetrate her.

Sniffing, tears on her cheeks, she glanced over her shoulder and found such a look of rage on the Alpha's face.

His hands, fingers spread, were hovering over the line of welts on her back.

Her only value in the eyes of Alphas was in her beauty, and she had already disgusted the one who possessed total power over her now.

Afraid, she sat a hip to the floor, pulled her knees under her chin, and made herself as small as possible. She even apologized. "I've been told they won't scar. You won't have to look at them forever."

Climbing to his feet, he stood over her, nostrils flared and eyes wild. When she began to cry, he bounded from the nest. The nearest piece of furniture was grabbed; the Alpha flipping a table with such strength it broke against the wall. Next, a chair sailed through the air, his roar louder than a dragon's when it shattered. After he'd torn a corner of the room to pieces, the brute flew, shouting at the top of his lungs, out the door.

14

Never in her life had Morgaine seen anything like it—that type of rage, that total loss of control.

The second she was alone, she darted from the foreigner's sleeping pit, threw on the shreds of her clothing, and grabbed the first potential weapon she could get her hands on.

A broken bit of metal, the edge sharp enough to cut into her palm as she gripped it.

The layout of his rooms was unfamiliar, but she ran through them looking for a decent place to hide or a way to get out. The wash chamber was too small, the room for food consumption too sparse. There was a living area with a view of space. In there, she saw they had left her planet, that a company of ships flew at their side.

The weight of it left her reeling.

She was alone in space, stupidly hiding in a dark room from a male whom she been given to like a sacrificial lamb.

…as if he'd *never* find her.

The ridiculousness was not lost. Morgaine looked down at the sharp sliver in her hand, saw the way she clutched the ruined dress over her breasts, and knew hopelessness.

Whatever he had in store for her, she could not stop it.

Running the back of her hand over flushed cheeks, she wiped the tears away, and straightened her shoulders to face him with the last bits of pride she could muster.

The sound of the Alpha returning could be heard in the other room. Swallowing back a sick feeling, she turned from the view, standing so he would see her when he checked this final room. It did not take him long.

Still naked, his flaccid cock hanging thick and foreboding between his legs, he strode in with a scowl. Shorter and less muscular, a fully dressed man followed and immediately averted his eyes.

This frazzled companion was clearly a Beta like the men in her settlement—the first Beta she had seen in days.

The Alpha began to speak, his voice low, calm,

almost poetic in its velvety meter. He even purred.

A moment later the Beta translated. "Our Heidron would like to know who struck you and why."

What did it matter? What did any of this matter?

Morgaine tightened her grip on her makeshift weapon, felt the skin on her palm split until warm blood dripped down the blade. When the Heidron sniffed the air and darted a glance to her hand, when it looked as if he prepared to approach, Morgaine narrowed her eyes, and growled at the pair of them. "I was taken from my mother, forced to endure *lessons* on how to be a proper Omega, threatened constantly with unwanted male attention, and watched every minute of every day. I was struck because I disliked it."

The words were fed back to the Alpha, the one watching her bleeding hand with his own narrow-eyed gaze. He did not find her answer satisfactory.

The Beta asked again. "Who struck you and why?"

Morgaine found the question pointless considering the brute who'd asked it, and snarled, "The day before you arrived, I laid down in the glass cage and ignored the rude questions and vulgar demands of the Alphas who came to bid on me. The commandant assured that I would not be able to sit or lie down again the next day. He ordered five strikes of a cane. The sergeant responsible for my transition carried out the sentence, adding in an extra strike for good measure. The Alpha with the greatest claim to me held me down, though he offered to take my punishment upon himself."

Every word was fed back to the one staring at her. His eyes went to hers when he spoke for the Beta to translate. "You smell like fear."

Her lip shook. "You're very scary."

"And you believe you can fend me off with that broken bit of metal?"

Morgaine glanced down at her bloody weapon. "No, but if I get you angry enough, you will kill me more quickly."

He paced toward her, pried the shard from her numb fingers, and threw it to crash against the nearest wall. "A weapon will not work unless you are willing to wield it, girl. I suggest never raising one to me again."

Taking her bleeding palm in his hand, he inspected the shallow wound.

The last traces of pride and bravery vanished when he licked it. "If you are angry about the marks on my back, I was assured they would not scar."

His palm cupped her cheek, fingers curling around her skull. A smear of her blood on his lips, he rumbled, the translation following. "I am angry about the wounds. Very angry. But I am not angry with you."

Unsure what to say, Morgaine closed her eyes, a

long breath leaving her chest. Again, he put her cheek to his chest, his hand to her hair, and placed an arm firmly around her middle.

The resonant purr was like warm sand for her to sink into. It felt treacherous and untrustworthy, even as it promised safety and warmth. Like the thing he'd done to her in his nest, the way he'd turned her body against her and made her the true definition of feral.

The male knew how to control in ways which Sergeant Uriel had only tested the waters and Corporal Esin had yet to learn.

Pressing closer to that noise, Morgaine muttered, "I don't know what to do."

The words had been too soft for the translator to hear, but the Alpha responded as if in perfect understanding, his Beta companion announcing, "He says you shall rest now."

The translator dismissed, Morgaine was taken back into the sleeping chamber. Only this time, she was not shoved into the bedding, but urged to lie down on her stomach. A short time later his weight came heavy beside her, a cool pass of medicine swabbed over her back and buttocks until her hurts vanished.

He talked again as if explaining all he did, bandaged her hand, stroked her hair. Morgaine passed into dreams anchored by the sound of a stranger's purr-rich voice, warmed by the heat of his body.

DARK HAIR SLIPPING over her bare skin like a brush of feathers, Simin took his time scent-marking his mate as she slumbered. The graze of his jaw over her alluring curves set bumps to smooth flesh and a soft smile to his kor'yr's mouth.

Males knew to purr, and yes, he had for other women in the past, but never as loud or as strong as he did for this one. She inspired an impressive, and it would seem necessary, amount of noise to echo from his ribs to sing her into a state of calm.

So much more docile in sleep, he adored every last inch of her.

She did not tense as he tasted her body, she did not smell of fear.

No, she smelled like sunshine.

He'd recognized her scent at once on the enemy ship, slipping into a heated rage when he saw she was imprisoned. He'd *saved* her from the weakling Nierra. Brought her to a nest where he would cherish and adore her. Where he would breed her. Where their younglings would be born.

Hours were spent exploring, soothing, and healing his overwrought conquest.

Carefully drawing one nipple into his mouth, he groaned at how she wriggled in her dreams. Her taste was pure decadence, and he could not find a favorite between them when he lapped at its mate. Licking between her toes had inspired the girl to arch her back in sleep, even her thighs had softly parted, giving him a view of that pretty, slick-smeared cunt.

Her resistance to his tasting her hours ago had been cute. The thing had no idea what he'd been about, surprised all the more when she'd liked it.

Whatever the Nierra did with their females, it sounded as bland as their battle technique—pomp backed by so little substance. The girl didn't know it yet, but life for her would be much better as his kor'yr no matter her hesitations or fear.

No matter if she found him ugly.

At least he knew how to fuck.

Speaking of fucking, he wanted to do so now—to slip inside her while she slept and wake her with a full belly of cock. She would like it, just as she'd liked his tongue on her clit. There was no question in Simin's mind.

Balls aching, he put a grip on the base of his shaft, stroking up hard enough to blend pain into pleasure. He could come just looking at her. Tempted to release over the sleeping Omega, to leave something sweet on her lips, Simin groaned.

Upon hearing his frustration, her left leg shifted in sleep, pussy opening to him in unspoken offering.

It was easy to balance over her body, to set his swollen crown against her eager slit.

A virgin they'd claimed, one about to get her first cock. She'd yelped under his tongue, screamed when she'd come. What would she do when she felt her first knot? He'd bet five ships and a planet of farmland she'd squeal.

Even in sleep, her body was responding to his low-pitched growls, the aroma of slick growing stronger by the minute. A simple tilt of his hips and his fat cockhead would pop inside that tight passage. One surge forward and he'd have her full to the brim.

His body moved with the thought, sloshing its way through her scented offering.

The pretty one's eyes flew open just as he breached, stretched, and claimed that tight hole.

So wet, so hot, smelling so fucking good, there was no question of how hard to rut.

One harsh, earsplitting howl, lips pulled back from his teeth, he thrust onward until he claimed all for himself.

The surprise on her face was as beautiful as the pulse of her cunt around his throbbing invasion.

He surged, shoved in deep, and felt perfection. "Kor'yr, I want to hear you scream again."

And she did. Only it wasn't a true scream as there was no noise when she threw back her head on a silent wail. The reek of her fear came back, just in time to excite the Alpha who would show her fear could flavor pleasure just as pain could heighten the thrill.

15

I t wasn't real, it couldn't be. Oh, but it felt jagged and raw, stretching out her insides in a way that seemed impossibly deep.

Her nails dug into warm biceps, Morgaine trying to hold on when the first cramp stole up her spine and left her reeling. His exceptional length didn't fit, and her body vehemently rebelled.

Still, he surged forward until powerful hips slammed against her.

No matter how rough his thrusts, the lips at her ear murmured softly. His meaning was lost, but his intention could not be missed. He sounded as if he were in even greater pain than she, that grainy voice tight, throttled, and shallow.

Squeezed around his searing invasion, she tried to drive him out, and only inspired him to moan in bliss.

When she panted in time to his rhythm, he praised her.

In a sunken bed that smelled sweet and equally strange, staring at the mosaic ceiling of a room as foreign to her as the male using her body, Morgaine understood exactly what Alphas were capable of.

It was like being dragged up a mountain, legs twisted and back bent. It was like being filled with writhing snakes and liquid gold. Cell by cell, sensation took over, locking her away in a part of her mind that was blurred by pleasure whether she'd invited it or not.

Her control was as cloudy as the Alpha's eyes, and then even that was taken from her.

Something changed in the shape of the shaft stabbing into her belly. It pulled, grew and caught at the mouth of her cunt.

A forming knot.

Just like the Omega she'd watched on the wall, Morgaine began to wail for release… and then it came. Everything inside her twisted, seized about his knot and pulled him into a belly sore from the stretch, yet needy for more.

When the first spurt of boiling seed sprayed her womb, she screamed.

There was no word for such feeling.

Another eruption of come, and she bit his bicep to keep from howling.

A third, a fourth, and she was certain her body would burst apart from the pressure of his spurting semen built up behind the knot.

His forehead came to hers, the male panting, "*Youvertr'kril, dorngut yaka nilie.*"

When the world stopped spinning, Morgaine found her hands had tangled in his hair. Holding to him, even her legs had wrapped around his waist.

She held on to him as if life itself could only be found in his embrace.

It was as Sergeant Uriel had claimed. Nothing in life had moved her as much as being mounted. Staring at the milky eyes shining down at her, knowing it could have been any Alpha… grasping that the males knew the power they might wield… turned what had been beautiful into something tarnished.

To be Omega was to be consumed, fed upon, and discarded.

Would it have felt different in the pleasure chambers, or would she have been dragged to such heights by male after male who'd paid Esin's fee? Where was the intimacy and love Uriel had spoken of?

Everything felt like a lie.

Running her hands from his shoulders, fingering muscled arms, Morgaine made herself learn the shape and texture of him, made herself recognize who he was and what he had done.

Inside her belly he was still hard as stone, and

when she moved her hips, she found her body locked to his. The knot persisted, tying them together. Exquisite as it was horrid.

It seemed wrong that she had enjoyed it, worse still that she would enjoy it time and time again. *They don't use you only once.* Uriel had made that clear. Esin had made that clear. The males who had gathered outside the glass cage had made that clear.

Heart breaking, she looked into the eyes of the man whose cock still twitched inside her and said her name. "Morgaine."

At first, he seemed to misunderstand, but then he smiled. "Simin. Heidron Simin Gralloch." A light kiss was pressed to her mouth. "Kor'yr Morgaine."

There was a ripple in her internal muscles, a tightening around his girth. As it happened, she watched Simin's eyes close on a sigh of pleasure. He was still in ecstasy, caught up in rapture as another wave of come was drawn from his body deep into hers.

Settling back against his cushions, she closed her eyes to wait it out and think of anything else.

Her apathy was unacceptable to the male, who rocked deeper against her, rubbing himself where she was tender, until she too was moaning.

When he licked his thumb and reached between their bodies to manipulate the nerves of her clit, it only took three strokes until she was climaxing again, whimpering as her insides went wild and as that invasive knot seemed to grow even larger.

He would not leave her alone.

When nature had decided their coupling was at an end, the knot shrank, a wave of fluid gushed from her body, and his still hard cock started the game all over again.

The Alpha took her five times, over and over, offering Morgaine no rest or escape from how he could make her body sing. When he was finally finished, he lay with his mouth near her breast, indolently toying with her nipple, chuckling every time he flicked his tongue over the pert tip, no matter how she whimpered.

Joints aching, Morgaine worked to extricate her body from the weighted limbs of a giant. And a giant he was—taller than Esin or Uriel, darker skinned too —scarred, rough, and unashamed of doing what he wished to her body without explanation or gentle suggestion.

If he wanted to feast between her legs, he did, regardless of their mixed fluids or her lack of a bath. When he wanted her on her knees, he put her there, and used her body to suit his tastes.

When he took the calmer route, her squirming never stopped his explorations.

Simin took what he desired, Morgaine unable to even communicate the simplest of refusals.

She told herself that was why she allowed all his pleasures. She lied.

He ruled her with so little effort, and for some reason, that made looking back on all that had been done disconcerting.

The Alpha, Simin, was breathing deep in sleep, his hands tangled in her hair. Slumber did not lend him a look of innocence. Not one bit. There was a reason this man had walked at the head of his people, a reason he had been the one speaking to the commandant.

A reason Uriel's men had spoken harshly of him in hushed tones when they thought she'd slept.

Doing her best to work her locks free of the strange Alpha's grip, Morgaine unwound the tangles with care, but he woke all the same.

Cloudy eyes blinked at her, the male watching as she slowly scooted back.

Smoothing her locks, trying not to grimace when movement brought discomfort, she made her way to the edge of the sleeping pit, all under a predator's gaze.

Fingers curling over the ridge of the bed, Morgaine pulled herself higher. But before she might escape completely, he sat up, cocked his head and scowled.

A series of grumbled words were offered, the male crawling toward her as if to capture an ankle and pull her body under his.

She drew away, shook her head, and said, "No."

He sounded out her word. "No?" He parroted the word a second time, "No," and it seemed to dawn on him what it meant.

Morgaine didn't speak his language any better than he spoke hers, but she thought to placate the male before he might punish her withdrawal. Pulling her arms tight around her middle, failing at offering a neutral smile, she chewed a lip and glanced toward the bathroom.

She might have been crusted with his dried come, but the Alpha narrowing his eyes bore marks of his own.

His blood was caked under her nails, just as his skin was covered in the scratches she'd put there. She'd even left the bite of her teeth on his arm and shoulder. But, there were bruises on her where the Alpha had grabbed too tight, her inner thighs were mottled, and between her legs thrummed an abiding ache.

Afraid that if she did not leave his nest he would try to mount her again, she startled when the male traced a finger down her thigh.

He said her name. "*Morgaine, clota via kan'nai.*"

Bladder near bursting and extremely thirsty, she dared to look in the direction of the washroom again.

Hands braced upon the edge of the bed, boxing her in, Simin rose, massive and looming. When she thought to scoot back, he took her upper arm and said her word, "No."

Climbing out of the nest with ease, he took her arm, helped her up, and led Morgaine exactly where she kept staring. At the door, he said a word that sounded like a sneeze. "*Achoo.*"

Staring through the portal straight at the toilet, she tried to brush him off.

He said, "No," squeezed her arm, and went in with her. He even sat her down on the toilet, no matter her hesitation. "*Achoo.*"

Urinating before she could stop herself, and absolutely hating the way he smiled down and pat her head, Morgaine dared to growl. It was as low and thoroughly annoyed as she could manage.

The jerk laughed, reaching between her legs to wipe her clean.

He was careful, but it stung both her pride and the place he had repeatedly knotted. Fingernails digging into his forearm, Morgaine hissed at the contact. She forced him off and gave the male a look that said if he touched her again she was going to hurt him.

Simin backed away.

Arms crossed over his chest, he cocked a brow, as if telling her to finish.

Frustrated, sore, upset about the lack of privacy in her life, Morgaine obeyed.

As soon as she was off the vessel, the Alpha brushed her aside, his flaccid member already in hand. As he took his turn, he put a hand to the wall, leaned forward, and threw back his head on a sigh.

Morgaine just stood there gawking. When he shrugged at her expression, she threw a hand over her eyes, rushed out of the room, apologizing as if she'd done something wrong.

He was after her in an instant, had her cornered against the wall, and there was no more laughter.

Bulk pressed her flat, immobile, and lips came to Morgaine's ear. Then silence.

Simin didn't speak. What he was doing or why, she could not make out. Trapped as she was, all she could see was the male's tense shoulders moving with his breaths.

Teeth set to her earlobe and on her sharp inhale, he bit down. Lower his head went, and then he bit her neck. No skin was broken, but the force of his jaw inspired an ache, the action pure warning. He was not toying with her, working to seduce, or even offering comfort.

He was telling the Omega who was in charge, who

was to be obeyed, and who held her very life in his jaws.

It was not until those sharp nips grazed her shoulder that light warning became rough action. There he set his mouth, licking a single spot clean. The flat of his tongue working, her skin growing pink, he drew out a flush.

One large hand took her jaw, angling her head, the other took a firm hold of her hip. Between their bodies, his cock grew hard and dripped the pearly warning that he was ready to fuck again.

No purr was offered to induce her calm.

He was all Alpha, she was cornered Omega, and his message was coming through loud and clear.

Do not run from me.

When Simin set his teeth to her flesh, he rolled his hips, using her belly for soft friction just as he bit down.

There was a promise in that sting, a promise sealed in the first blood he drew. Though shallow, his mark was there, and her pain was real.

Still holding the Omega's shoulder in his teeth, he made a grab for her hand, and pulled it between them.

A calloused palm closed her small fingers around a thick cock and guided her to stroke hard and quick. He grunted with the movement, breath growing shallow, making her participate in his pleasure until he burst milky white over heaving tits and fluttering belly to drip down bruised thighs.

Painting her with ejaculate, growling his release, he dragged her touch down to the growing knot and forced her to squeeze. And still he came, jettisoning more cream over and over the girl trapped by his teeth.

I own you. You will obey. You will smell of me. I can make you like it.

What they had shared in pleasure, any trace of awe Morgaine might have fostered, died right then.

Esin would have treated her the same way.

16

"You are perfection." Simin had made a lovely mess of his trembling mate—the lightly bleeding wound atop her shoulder not quite as glorious as the future claiming mark would be, but extremely appealing nonetheless. So delicious; he could not stop tasting it. Lower, her perky tits dripped with his latest ejaculate, come beading atop pink nipples.

What he'd give to have her reach down and gather those droplets, to watch her bring them to her tongue to swallow in delight.

The thought made him spill one last, half-hearted spurt of seed, greasing the flesh between them when Simin pressed even closer. Lost in her scent, working his mass against her gentle form in a blatant, seductive attempt to rub as much of his spend into her skin as possible, he failed to notice.

Until she made a terrible whimper.

His mate was… crying.

Heart falling, squeezing as if caught in a vise, his cock went soft before Simin opened his eyes and found the *opposite* of what such giving actions should have inspired.

Sad eyes, beautifully blue but bloodshot with terrible emotion, were turned away.

This would not do. Even now the air was growing bitter with Omega fear and salty with spilled tears.

"I have waited an age, set aside many eager, ranked Omegas in search of my kor'yr. For you." Determined, brusque he spoke words none but her would ever hear. Words he would have killed any male or female for witnessing. Private mutterings between mates, an open display of weakness and exaltation, unheard of from any Heidron. Gathering her hand, he pressed it where his purr resonated strongest —right over his heart. "There is nothing you ever need fear from me."

The female blinked once, her shoulders slumped, and she appeared… resigned.

Dark circles under her eyes, golden hair lank, bathed in the drying remnants of his sperm, and smelling of the sweet honey that dripped between her legs, she looked worn but resplendent.

Pained to watch her flinch when his hand came to cup her cheek, Simin murmured, "Did the Nierra not take care of you? Did they put poison in your mind?"

She couldn't answer, was ignorant to his words and their meanings, leaving Simin with no way to encourage her affection outside of action. So he took a step back and waited for her to find the courage to meet his eyes.

At first she continued to stand as she was, shrinking in on herself, unsure, with the shallow breaths of a frightened rabbit. But when she began to realize we waited, a very timid, very tired set of eyes traced their way over his impressive body before landing on an open gaze that waited. For her.

He smirked, reaching out to trill his fingers over the twin crescents his teeth had punctured into her flesh.

And she… she looked utterly confused.

Horrified.

Sick.

"We have had much sex play. You must be hungry." Trailing his touch down her arm, he found her fingers and threaded them with his. "Come this way. I shall feed you. I will wash you. I will lay you down in our nest, take you gently, and give you strong arms to sleep in until your eyes shine and your smiles are easy."

He gave her a gentle tug and led her from a room

that reeked of their sex, her fear, and his concern, guiding her to his private dining quarters. Once there, after sitting her in his favorite chair and stepping a goodly distance away, Simin saw her visibly relax.

It wasn't only the starscape glimmering from the view portal that had her attention, it was the fact that her new mate had walked away.

As Heidron of a prime fleet, as a seasoned warrior with many conquests under his belt, Simin was unaccustomed to feeling lacking. Women threw themselves at him, he'd laid with hundreds and took great pride in his proficiency with female pleasure.

His body was large, muscular, pleasing. He didn't have the finest features, but endurance, patience, even in tactical skills he was wiser than even the eldest of his brothers. Favored by his mother for his humor.

Yet his kor'yr, the Omega his soul resonated for, did not wish to be near him.

She did not recognize him…

Scowling at the meat he folded around seasoned paste, he growled. From the corner of his eye, even with her all the way across the room, his mate jumped. And once again the air went sour with female fear.

This was not right.

She might not understand his words, but intention could be communicated.

Nothing was unsalvageable, especially between and Alpha and Omega so deeply connected. Careful of his tone, but lacking the charisma of a sweeter man, Simin's deep voice carried over the room. "To be the mate of Heidron is a great honor. Every soldier in my fleet would lay down his life for yours. You have nothing to fear in my presence. I won't correct you with a cane."

Watching him, infinitely wary, his Morgaine blinked, rubbed her lips together and nodded as if trying to please him. But once her eyes fell on the food in his hands, she shot from her seat and rushed forward.

Hands coated in the raw juices of fine *bolx* meat, fingernails smeared with paste, he didn't stop her. In fact, Simin didn't know what to make of her frantic expression when she saw that he was preparing them food. Hunger had not draw her to him.

Terror had.

Reaching for meat, she looked at the slices he had already prepared and mimicked the simple preparation so quickly the plate was full, messy, and complete before he knew how to react. She then pushed it closer to him.

Was she offering him the food he had chosen for her?

She was, and blue eyes frantic as if she'd done wrong in sitting while he worked.

"It's for you. Alphas serve their mates before they serve themselves."

She pushed the plate again, eyeing the mess of her work as if she knew she could have done better. Cringing as if she expected to be punished.

Careful to choose one she had made, Simin lifted it up and nodded confused approval.

Morgaine smiled, a tight practiced movement that did not reach her eyes. A smile that fell off her lips when he held out the bite for her to eat from his hand. She didn't so much as sniff it, probably didn't even taste it, avoiding his fingers to take it into her mouth and swallow without chewing.

And then she mirrored what he'd done, speaking her fluid tongue as if profusely apologizing as she held up a bite of the delicacy for him.

Wrapping her wrist in his much larger hand, he plucked the treat from her fingers and returned it to the plate. Then he escorted her back to the best seat, took it for himself, and patted his knee so she might join him.

Expression blank, she stiffly obeyed, her slick-drenched pussy smearing sweet fluid over his hard thigh. He pulled her close when it grew painfully obvious she was going to try to balance herself like a perched bird instead of fitting herself to him. The arm he hung around her, the light stroking of her skin, didn't soften her ramrod spine, nor did it earn so much as a hum of approval from the woman.

His purr increased, his body pliant.

Patience was imperative to battle strategy. Before so much as a drop of blood was shed, the enemy was to be studied, their patterns analyzed, their psyche broken down into its basic parts and used against them. Though he'd never had to woo a woman to gain her attention, his course would be no different than planning war.

All wars he waged he won.

Taming his Omega would be no different.

Simin gave her time to find a comfortable position as his purr softened her tension, a gentle stroke caressing her arm. And then he fed her, slowly. Offering only enough that she'd have to bite off manageable pieces, cooing nonsense words of encouragement—vibrating with pleased groans when her tongue caught his fingers. But each time she tried to lift a piece for him, he took it from her and put it back on the plate.

There could be reciprocation in the future once she knew him better and understood his intrinsic craving to care for her. Once she was at peace in his presence and in love with his heart.

There would be love.

And children who would please his mother and even make his dour father crack a smirk when he thought no one was looking.

When she chewed even slower and a bulge bumped from her belly from too much food, he fed himself the scant remainder on the plate. Eyes on the view, content and growing more confident in his approach, he spoke of all their lives would be and confessed that he'd been lonely for her, had made great, secret offerings to the higher power so he might find her... wondering to himself if he was only willing to admit it aloud because she could not understand and think less of his prowess for unmasculine sentimentality.

Every Alpha desired an Omega mate, but to find a kor'yr was something not one in a billion might accomplish. Simin had found his propped up in a glass cage as if the gods themselves had set her aside for him.

The arm around her supple body grew tighter, pressing them into one being.

HE HAD FED her raw meat. *Raw*.

Morgaine still wanted to cringe just thinking of it. Did these people not know of parasites and bacteria that could rage through a colony and massacre half a settlement? One bad well had poisoned over twenty people when Morgaine had still been a child.

A single wrong sip of water. Dysentery. Burial.

Yet he had partaken in the meal when she was painfully full with smiling lips and sounds of satisfaction. The juxtaposition of this place and their barbaric customs set her head spinning. He looked like a savage, spoke like one, yet possessed the finest rooms she'd ever seen.

That plate was bone china, if not some kind of cut milky crystal. The furnishings were immaculate.

Where was the leather, the bones, the carcasses of his latest kill roasting over an open fire?

How did the male who shattered the glass of her enclosure, who had penetrated her the first time while she still slept, equate with *this*?

How did he know how to touch her to make her mindlessly spread and howl for more?

When was he going to mutilate her? In what ways?

Would he kill her after? Share her?

What was she going to do?

Dizzy with horrible, circular thoughts, the pounding behind Morgaine's eyes grew. The male was still talking, his ugly language croaked so deep the one speaking sounded like a cross of a toad and a thunderstorm. And as he talked, he touched.

Light strokes to her brow, across her cheeks, running those calloused fingers between her bared breasts to jostle her ribs until she jumped. No coerced laugh broke past her lips, Morgaine determined to bear the tickling rather than face his ire.

Because her life was in his hands and she was so

thrown by the last few days—by the pain that still lingered muscle deep where a cane had lashed her, and the loss of everything she knew—that she had no idea where to turn.

Her cunt, and that was the name it had been reduced to, ached. And even aching, it still wept that horrible fluid.

Part of her even wanted this awkward meal to end so he might take her back to the nest and twist her mind back into that stark white place of feeling. That place where she forgot her name, her inhibitions, where she felt free in the loss of who she was because there was nothing to mourn if she was nothing at all.

Scarred, older than any courting boy she'd received flowers from, older than even grabby Esin. His fingers still sticky with the parts of her body they had delved into and the raw meat they had shared, the crazed male Sergeant Uriel and his commandant had given her to, smiled. It was lopsided but displayed healthy teeth too straight to be natural.

Back home, dentistry was expensive. Morgaine was missing a molar near the back that had gone rotten in her teen years. Tonguing the empty space, a little self-conscious her teeth were a bit crooked, she felt even worse for such shallow concerns. It wasn't her teeth this man wanted her for.

It was the deceptive slut of a slit between her legs.

17

Who could imagine it would be so difficult to bathe a single, tiny female? Especially one who clearly needed the relaxation of a deep soak, warm water, fresh soap, and doting hands to tend where she was most likely sore. They had fucked a great deal, and no male of his worth—even in the deepest rut—would allow his mate to grow filthy with crusting fluids.

Considering that she was an untried virgin who had let him do as he desired, Simin was doubly sure she could use the luxury.

Yet his kor'yr had grown so agitated with the experience she'd started to grind her teeth and leak silent tears. It had come to the point he'd let her break tradition and wash him just to keep her from losing the tattered remains of her failing composure.

The feel of her hands on his body had been wonderful, but the very significant reason she did it was *anything* but pleasurable.

Every time he moved, she flinched as if preparing to accept a strike.

Where was the wildcat who'd grabbed up a piece of sharp debris days ago?

If I get you angry enough, you will kill me more quickly.

Those had been her words when the Beta translator had been summoned.

Maybe he had not taken her words as seriously as he should have. Relying on their bond to ease her considerable distress, spoiling her with gratuitous fucking—it had changed nothing.

She was more skittish now than when he had brought her home.

Simin even wondered what she would do if given the opportunity to leave. Would she flee, seek another protector? Would she hate him as it seemed she did now?

This was beyond fear. This was spiritually unhealthy.

A featherlight skim of fingertips traced the outline of his shoulders, his Omega seeking out the spaces where muscles met so a practiced touch might knead tension away. God how he tried to be pliant, to soften all that musculature so she might be done with her unnecessary show of… servitude.

Someone had trained her to do this—trained her so deeply she could not allow him to bathe her until she had satisfied some unknown ritual.

There was no give and take, she would not even allow him to wash her beyond a quick scrub of her chest.

Simin wanted to touch her in this way, to knead the tension from her knotted muscles, to ease her into deserved contentment. No Nierra slave he'd taken to bed had ever acted in this compulsory way his mate did. Some were skittish—many slaves were—but this was…

What had they done to so wonderful an Omega?

Irritated by his unruly imagination and the horrible things he knew his vanquished enemy capable of, he took the sponge from her fingers, barking an order for her to cease scrubbing him and sit back.

It was the exact wrong thing to say.

She withered. She who had been so determined to show him this *thing* she could do.

Female skin going green, watching her throat work, Simin was certain she was going to be sick. His own mouth watered with the sour precursor of vomit just seeing his mate so ill.

"Kor'yr, you did well." *Insulting tradition by*

washing me first. "But I am Alpha and you are Omega. I provide and you accept. In exchange, you give me great joy by cherishing our pair-bond and nest."

The sunken tub could have housed five grown warriors of merit, offered enough space to frolic, to rinse, and to relax, even to fuck if they wanted too. But now it was a big bowl of steaming misery.

There was no joy here because she was blind, blue eyes brimming with sorrow, and skin sweating with fear.

And he was failing.

Purr stilted by shoulder deep water, Simin stood so the female might feel the true depth of the comforting sound he offered and approached where she'd sunk low. Chin skimming the water, golden hair floating about her like spun tentacles of sunshine, she gazed up.

She gazed up and looked utterly lost.

It crushed him, enraged him, and stirred up a searing burn behind his ribs he'd never known before. Cupping that chin under the water, drawing her to sit up, to present herself, he took care to wash, massage, tend and soothe every part of her in a gentle pantomime of sex. Of adoration and solace. Simin did everything he could to express how he wished her to be happy.

And she stank of misery the whole time. Worse, she tried to lie by smiling, chirping out her language the more he frowned.

When he took her back to their nest, he broke his word and did not take her body as he'd said he would. Instead he laid her head upon a pillow of green silk, covered her with the smooth slip of satin, and purred at her side until she slept.

Then he slunk away.

While she slept, he found all the shattered pieces scattered in his rampage and hid them out of sight. He cleaned like a lowly slave. He prepared food so that when she woke it would be ready and there would be no awkward, wordless fight over who would make it.

He sat before his view of space and pondered deeply.

And for the first time since he'd brought her into their home, she slept the whole night through. She slept, he knew, because he was far away.

"I will fix this." A vow from a Heidron was unbreakable.

"I FEED HER, heal her, pet her, wash her—I have given the Omega days on end of my company." Simin stood stolid at the threshold of an unwelcoming portal,

Morgaine wide-eyed, tense, and glued to his side.
Before them, an old woman, one blocking the way forward even as Simin made his plea, did not so much as smile. "Omega Superior, I have knotted her so many times she has passed out. The stink of fear has not diminished. Her desire has not once urged her to reach for me in comfort. My kor'yr does not recognize me."

The gatekeeper looked to the girl in question as she clung to his arm, and Simin knew she found more than the smell of anxiety hanging in the air. She saw the same broken look in cerulean blue eyes that he had. The golden-haired outsider was cloaked in a look of soul-dead hopelessness, cowering behind her Alpha as if to hide from one unknown female, yet terrified of them both.

Though small in stature as Omegas were, the elder female was large in presence. "A pair-bond will crush her misgivings and shape her affection to your will. Why bring her here when you are in full rut and she smells close to her time?"

To be questioned was not something a Heidron—a favored Omari Prince—was accustomed to. Nor were conversations of such private matters openly held in the halls of his squadron's flagship. "She does not speak our language, was a virgin in captivity before I freed her. Upon her retrieval, repeatedly the Nierra referred to her as *feral*. I do not know what this means. I do know that she was beaten under their care for refusing."

"Refusing what?"

"Male attention."

Dressed in loose robes in the same style as Simin's unhappy mate, the Omega Superior warned, "You take a risk in bringing her here still lacking a pair-bond, Heidron. Your rule does not extend past this door. The Omegas might not give her back to you."

"Do not speak to me as if I were some pup!" The snap in his voice did not move the gray-haired woman blocking the portal, but behind the Alpha, his mate startled and made a horrible noise. Immediately increasing the already loud vibration resonating just to soothe her, Simin growled, "Her needs come before my own. I have tried and failed to reassure her. I cannot tolerate the smell of another male in my rooms, even to help translate. An Omega so near her nest at this point would be a threat to her. And even if I had the luxury of sharing our words, I do not think she will tell me the true way of things. Look at her; she's frightened, even of you. I seek assistance. Return her to me smiling and eager to know her kor'yr, and the tithe I will offer in exchange will buy worlds."

"Your riches mean nothing to us." The woman offered a sardonic half grin, stepped back and swept her arm to the side. "But, by all means, lead her inside."

Trouble began the instant they were through the unadorned door and a gallery of opulent color, of embroidered cushions, of laughter, of trays of rich food, and nothing but beautiful females came into view.

Morgaine began to lowly keen.

Simin's foreign Omega began to frantically rattle off in her language, to plead in a tone that set the women in the room to their feet. Holding onto the Alpha's arm, she dug in her heels in a sorry attempt to slow his steps, and then she fell to her knees, weeping so mournfully he did not know how to calm her.

Female arms clasped around bulky male thighs, sobbing, Morgaine refused to let him go. He had to pry her off, forced to ignore her terror, and leave her under the care of those Omegas who had rushed forward to help.

Morgaine began to scream.

He could do nothing for her now, not when there was a golden tiled mark on the floor designating how far an Alpha might tread in that sacred room. To cross that line meant instant death. The Omegas would kill him, whether he was their Heidron or no.

Unable to bear watching his mate be bodily dragged away, he turned his back, obeying the Omega Superior's orders to leave at once.

Never had he imagined he'd see that old battle-axe startled.

THERE WAS no chance in the twelve hells that Simin would return to his rooms. He waited outside the door of the Omega sector for hours on end. At first, he'd heard his kor'yr screaming even through the thick metal portal. Caught up in the sound of her fear, he'd tried to get back in, to rush to her, but the females had wisely sealed the gate.

And then silence.

Even with his ear pressed to the door, he heard nothing.

A great warrior was to be patient, but for those hours waiting, he was anything but. Pacing, sitting, standing at attention—nothing helped.

He'd never expected Morgaine to respond as she had. Though he should have suspected when she was unimpressed, and then flat out shaking at his first offering of fine clothes. Clothes he'd had specially made in his family's colors and crests. Clothes crafted from the finest silks and encrusted with gems worthy of a Heidron's mate.

She had backed away from the folded green fabric, shaking her head, as if she knew he was dressing her only to take her away from the nest.

Flat out ignoring when he'd called her name, she'd started pointedly cleaning the nearest item she could reach… with her hair.

Gentle as he could be, he'd forced her to stop, dressed her, and took her straight to this place that left his mate broken and sobbing.

And now he could not even see her. Without the pair-bond, he could not feel her. Utterly at a loss, he felt an unprecedented stinging behind his eyes, and hung his head.

Then the door opened.

It was not his mate waiting for his attention, but a young Omega of rank—a translator by the marks on her robes.

Abrupt, he demanded, "Tell me."

The woman smelled shaken in her own right, but did her best to appear calm. "Morgaine is under the belief that you have brought her to something the Nierra refer to as *pleasure chambers*… that you have grown bored of her and left her here to be used at will by other males willing to pay your fee. I do not think I need to describe what she anticipated would be done to her in these rooms."

Simin's face went ashen. "What?"

There was much to explain and the hall was not a proper location for what had to be shared. The Omega, her hair shorn close to her skull as a sign she refused to take a mate, led him to a small waiting room and gestured for him to sit.

When he obeyed, she sat across from his bulk, smoothed her robes and was openly trying not to tremble. "The pleasure chambers were to be her fate for at least two years had she remained in Nierra care. In fact, it was the fate required by the male who was to have her for mate. By their law, he could not pair-bond to her until his rank had increased. After gathering powerful supporters, the weight of his claim outweighed all potential rivals. She learned of this while on display for the males already signing up for their turn. They made demands to see her body, growled to encourage her arousal against her will. She was shamed."

The glass cage was a bidding area? The defeated soldiers in the Nierra's ship, the ones he'd paraded naked before to shame them with his utter lack of fear had been signing up to abuse his kor'yr? How had he not considered this? Her clothing had been there, it was the reason he knew just what waited in that cage.

The scent of her had wafted toward him even in a sea of the enemy's stink. For the first time in his years, he had lost composure before his men. It had taken the whole mob to drag him from the enemy's ugly chambers.

He'd maimed males he'd known his whole life. For this woman.

To get to her. To care for her. To take her to his heart and tie them in a pair-bond that would be sung of throughout the ages.

The fire in Simin's eyes when he snarled at the wispy translator confirmed the threat. "I'll destroy every last Nierra, see their women despoiled and make slaves of their people. As of this moment, the treaty is dust."

"There is more."

Forcing his rage to quiet so he might know everything, Simin swallowed, steadied his breath, and demanded, "Tell me."

The nervous habit of running her fingers through her short brown hair showed itself for the third time. "The things they taught her, that they made her watch..."

This Omega was outside of her sanctuary, snapable neck within his reach. "Tell. Me."

So shaken was the woman that she failed to see the very real threat before her. "I do not even know how to describe the damage that was done, Heidron." She closed her eyes, openly disturbed. "Morgaine has no concept of estrous. She believes a pair-bond is equivalent to sex, and that all interaction she has shared with you *any Alpha could inflict on her*. Before today, she had never even seen another Omega. She... was told you would mutilate and rape her."

Foreign women were not protected by the Omari

code of honor, and such things did happen in war. In battle, any subjugate people could be taken as slaves. Once under ownership, new stock was protected from savagery. An Omari cardinal rule existed. Omegas could never be enslaved, only pair-bonded, and yes, often by force at the onset of estrous. But, from the moment the bond was established, they were considered Omari citizens under the protection and care of their mate.

The mateless Omega before him continued. "She thinks you bite her when she's done something wrong."

That could not stand. Voice unbearably sad, hardened by pent up rage, the Heidron snarled, "I mark her to reassure her that when estrous arrives I will forge the bond. It was done to make her feel safe in moments of her fear. It was done so she would know to trust me."

Compassion glimmered in the upturned golden eyes of the woman across from him. "We know… but that does not change our verdict."

Simin's expression turned deadly. "She's mine."

"She does not recognize you."

Rising to his feet, vibrating with the need to rend the Omega messenger limb from limb, Simin curled his lip. "I am Heidron of this fleet, your prince, and I will challenge the Omegas to have my kor'yr returned to me."

Brave, unflinching like the best Omari woman, the Omega stood her ground. "A handful of days ago she was taken by force from her mother. This was after years of evading the Nierra who raided her village. She fought through the pain of pre-estrous out of hatred of Alphas and love for the woman who birthed her. She suspected they would one day take her, she didn't know why, but she knew it was only a matter of time. In punishment for hiding her daughter, the mother's face was disfigured with a brand and Morgaine was listed as feral." Smoothing her robes then her hair, the Omega sat back, displaying so much sadness that even the enraged Alpha took notice. "Having spoken to her, it is an apt term. She is completely wild, totally ignorant, and indeed very scared."

Grinding his teeth, already imagining how best to bleed this woman, Simin hissed, "Why do you think I brought her to you?"

"We will allow you to court her for one hour each day."

"That is not even enough time to pleasure and knot her!"

Standing, meeting the eyes of her king's fifth son, she said, "Sex will not be allowed unless Morgaine initiates it."

They both knew that would never happen. Smoothing dark hair off his face, chest expanding in a full breath, Simin stared her down. "Until she learns our language, I have no way to communicate with her outside of physical acts. What am I supposed to do? Sit here and stare at her?"

"You claim she is your kor'yr." The Omega translator had done her duty, and chose to stand, leaving the room in a soft swish of robes. "Prove it."

18

———

"This will be your cubicle." The woman with hair shorn as short as the men wore theirs back in her settlement, Etaine, led her forward. Eyes shaded the verdant green of new grass were framed by an expression of shame, as if the woman thought the huge room disgraceful. "My apologies that it is not grander. Omegas who live within these halls choose an austere life."

Twice as large as Morgaine's cottage, this *cubicle* was full of many wondrous things. Walls that glowed just like the *first* ship she'd been forced to live in. But these walls were not reflective, only warm and slightly buzzing under her hand. And there was even a separate area for sanitary purposes similar in style to the one in the Alpha's quarters, only smaller and much more comfortable.

Because it was private.

For sleeping, she was assigned a cot—narrow, covered in fabric—and not an open pit in the center of the room.

The Omegas offered all this after Morgaine had clawed many of them with her nails, kicked several when they'd held her down, and even bitten one until she'd broken skin.

It was too good to be true. Fiddling with her battle-tangled locks, Morgaine asked again, "And you're going to let me stay? He can't come in here?"

"You are welcome here." Ever patient, Etaine answered the question for the tenth time. "And no, our Heidron cannot enter. No males are allowed to pass the Omegas' sacred golden line."

"It's just a mark on the ground. What's to stop them?"

Her guide didn't blink. "Those who have dared, we've killed. It is against every law to intrude upon Omegas gathered in their consecrated space."

A snort, half amused and half disbelieving, stuck in her nose. The women in this place were small like her. They were no match for an Alpha.

An elegant brow arched over what were probably the prettiest eyes Morgaine had even seen, Etaine challenging, "You don't believe me?"

"I have seen Alphas do terrible things." Cold despite the room's gentle warmth, Morgaine shivered.

"When I fought back, I lost. They made me do whatever they wanted."

"Our Heidron? Did he force you?"

It was a serious question; one Morgaine was unsure how to answer. Now that it had been explained to her what *Heidron* stood for, desperate to remain with the Omegas and far away from their prince, she vacillated. "I don't know."

And she didn't. She'd never fought back, but that didn't mean he had not taken liberties that had he asked, she would have refused.

Etaine offered what Morgaine suspected was a rare smile. "I'm glad you're with us. Not all Omegas desire Alpha attention. There are many here who understand how you feel."

Those words, a single shy smile, and Morgaine felt a weight lift from her shoulders. "Like you?"

"I am proud to be Omari. Proud to be Omega. For pleasure, I enjoy the attention of worthy males, but I do not wish for a mate. My career is my calling."

Many considered it tedious work, but Morgaine had loved weaving. Just as she had enjoyed her garden, the chickens, and goats. "I can sew clothes. Mend for the women here."

"If you like."

But what about sunlight on her face or the feel of a brisk breeze? "He's not going to let me go home, is he?"

"Never. It would be impossible." Etaine became serious, those green eyes aglow. "Be who and what you will in these rooms. Rest. Cry, if you need to. *Learn.* But should you cross that golden line, he will not give you up. Heidron Simin Gralloch values you highly, and has chosen you for his mate."

Morgaine didn't want him. "But I can stay here?"

"Forever, if that's how you desire to spend your life."

It was a start. Smiling, Morgaine thanked the women, unsure if she was to hug her or offer a hand.

"Get some rest. Food and supplies will be sent. I'll come for you tomorrow."

"Tomorrow?"

"Yes, the Heidron is to be allowed one hour of your presence each day. I will translate."

Panic, stomach-cramping terror. Of course this was too good to be true. "But I thought…"

"He brought you to us because he knew you suffered. He will wish to see that you're doing well… and Heidron Simin desires to court you."

THE DOOR to Omega Sector was due to be unbarred any moment now, and on the other side, his female would be waiting. A single night without her in their nest had set his teeth on edge.

There were no warm curves to hold close. No soft sighs as he pleasured her. There was nothing but her lingering scent to remind him that he'd ever even had her.

When slaves were summoned to scrub his quarters, he forbid them from disturbing the nest. Morgaine's presence must not be allowed to fade from the cushions. Burrowing in the bedding, breathing deeply of her scent was the only thing keeping him sane.

He had already considered five different methods of tearing down the Omega Sector door, ready to barge in and demand they return her to him.

He could cut off their air, refuse them supplies until they starved. Without crossing their fucking line, he could have her back.

But she would hate him even more than she already must.

The rut was working on his mind so powerfully that he thought he could even hear her soft mutterings if he closed his eyes hard enough and held a slick-stained pillow to his nose and breathed in until his lungs burned. Cock hard as an iron bar, he'd taken himself in hand. No matter how he milked his knot, there had been no relief. His balls ached, the hand working his shaft drawing out every last drop of come until he'd begun to climax dry.

It was agony.

Agony it would seem he deserved.

The Omega Etaine had been ordered to compile an expedited report on all Morgaine had shared. What Simin found projected before him pushed him past rage and into an emotion he could not name.

Flayed, stripped down to cracked bone and insignificant soul.

He had the names of Alphas, he had their rank, knew what ship they belonged to. In time he would have their lives. But first, he needed to help his kor'yr recover.

The best, most coveted foods were sent to Omega Sector to tempt her to eat. Fine clothes, jewels, anything a female might desire. Rare sweets.

She needed to see that he could provide anything she might desire, to learn that as a mate she would want for nothing.

His father once presented his wife the severed hands of an enemy tribe who had harmed her cousin. Simin would give Morgaine severed heads, the male's flaccid cocks jammed into their mouths, all atop a tray of pure gold.

He'd buy her the cleverest slaves to amuse her.

If she wanted a planet, he'd give her three.

That damn door between him and his mate *finally* began to open.

Morgaine already waited for him, but hovered out of reach past the forbidden demarcation of Omega space. It didn't matter. At least he could see her, smell her… maybe even touch her if she took just one more step forward.

Smiling, utter relief calming the bubbling agitation that had been burning the back of his throat, Simin entered. Their eyes met, he purred, but she did not return his joy.

Instead, she took a step backward and darted a nervous glance to the Omega with cropped hair waiting nearby.

His nervous bride spoke, her flittering language made solid by the translator. "I have been told that you are not allowed to cross this line."

The damned golden tile track between them held Morgaine's attention. Blue eyes so expressive in the throes of passion, refused to rise up and meet her mate's after their single fleeting shared glance.

Walking forward into a room sour with female fear, Simin rubbed at his chest where her fear stung him most. He wanted so badly to reach out and take her hand, but for his every step forward, she took another step back. "I'm not."

Morgaine was not adorned in any of the fine robes he sent to her, but wearing a style of dress Simin had never seen. It was plain, comprised of white fabric, and modest. "Did you make this garment?"

"Yes, Etaine"—Morgaine glanced to the translator

facilitating speech between them, smiling—"offered me some supplies."

"It's very pretty." But not what he had given her. Why was she not wearing what he had given her?

Hinting at a blush, Morgaine smoothed her skirt. "My mother taught me to sew, to weave, and to dye fabric. It was not considered a useful skill to the Alphas. None of my skills were. But here I've already collected a basket of items that require mending."

Cutting a sharp look toward the translator—allowing the heavy, penetrating nature of that glare to speak for him—Simin flat out threatened her. Mending was the labor of slaves, not queens. But… Morgaine spoke of her work with pride.

Furthermore, it was nice to hear about her. Daring to step forward to toe the dividing line, he coaxed, "Tell me of your talents."

Morgaine seemed embarrassed, cheeks turning pink as her eyes went back to the floor. "In my settlement, I was known for the quality of dyes I could produce… for fabric."

"And are you going to dye this dress? My household's colors are green." He was too eager, desperate to gain a glance. "I can find what you need… if you like. You would look beautiful in green."

She did not answer his offer. Speaking in a defensive tone even he could pick up without knowing her language, she carried on, "I raised fine goats and made cheese. Built houses, kept a garden. I was educated by farmers."

"Did you have many friends?"

She blinked and finally raised her head. "Aren't you going to mock me? *I said farmers.* I didn't even know how to work the door panel on this ship until Etaine showed me."

"You are industrious and, from the amount of skill I can already see worked into your gown, talented. Ascertaining the workings of this ship will come quickly to a mind keen to learn. The universe would do well to remember the endless labor of those who live simply."

She didn't know what to make of his answer, stared at him as if measuring his words and looking for the jibe.

"Tell me of your friends." Simin gave her a smile, the kind he used to win over his mother and steal treats as a child. "Tell me about your homeland. I want to know about my kor'yr."

A ghost of a smile changed Morgaine's face from pinched to considering. "My friends… well, I used to have many friends. As I got older, it grew difficult."

And one could easily sort out the reason. "Because you are Omega and the males wanted to be more than your friend?"

"I suppose…" Shaking her head and seemingly lost in thought, Morgaine confessed, "We had nursery rhymes about Omegas. It was not a thing anyone would want to be."

She was wrong. "To be born Omega is a blessing!"

Simin's passion behind his outburst did not impress her. She took another step back, lower lip beginning to tremble. "What do you know of it? It is terrible, and now that I've seen what happened to Esmerelda I understand why."

"Who?"

Etaine explained, sparing Morgaine from repeating what she'd confessed she'd been forced to watch. She told him of the lesson, of the bodies, how it had been her first time seeing a naked male. About the blood and fluids and nightmares.

Every last cell in his body urged him to step forward and go to his mate. Instead Simin retreated one step. Breathing heavily, reeking of anger, he put a hand to his eyes. "That was not Esmerelda's fault. How could she know the risks of estrous if she didn't know what she was? If anything, it was the fault of the Betas for a lack of self-control. But ultimately the blame is on the Alphas who created a situation in which such a thing might happen in the first place."

Morgaine went still, met his eyes, and had no words.

Simin had words. Many, many words in fact. "The Alphas showing you these things were employing psychological warfare. It's a common tactic used to twist enemy populations' thinking into the aggressor's design. It simplifies invasion."

Muttering, the golden-haired girl said, "They told me Alphas loved Omegas, that they existed to protect them. That all of it was for my own good."

The look on her face gutted him. Simin needed to hold her, but could offer only a purr. "They lied to you."

"I know. Otherwise they would not have threatened to whip my mother if I continued to disobey." Morgaine nodded, and looked utterly sad. "They never loved me at all."

Eager, Simin stood tall, reached out a hand in hopes she take it, and proclaimed, "I love you, kor'yr."

His movement sent her skittering back. "You don't know me!"

It had not been near an hour, but Morgaine turned around and rushed away from the prince who was contemplating risking death just to embrace her.

19

Powerless to stop her, Simin could do nothing but watch Morgaine rush out of sight. To say that their first meeting in this place had not gone as he'd hoped was a laughable understatement. He'd frightened her off even though he'd bared himself to ridicule by announcing a public declaration of his adoration.

Many prized Omari Omega mates went an entire lifetime without hearing so much as an *I love you* from their Alphas. Affection was demonstrated with action, with the quality of offerings and attention.

Devotion was demonstrated with attentive and vigorous fucking.

Never words.

Rumor would spread that he had bluntly declared his heart and she had denied his offering. Many of his men would snicker. Some might outright challenge him for weakness.

Simin did not care. He cared that he had frightened her.

He cared that she was distrusting of men, that the enemy had cheapened the power of that monumental word. And that wherever she'd gone to hide, that she was surely crying.

Because of him.

Riddled with frustration, with the undeniable effects of the rut—with a throbbing cock that would not lie down no matter how he abused it—he turned on the translator, vicious, angry, and… disappointed.

Had the short-haired Omega been wiser, she too would have retreated beyond the dividing line. Instead she straddled it. Easy prey.

Looking to her prince and not the retreating Omega, Etaine offered an appropriate bow. "My Heidron."

Biting back the roar already trying to rip from his chest, he grabbed her arm, and hauled her away from that blasted line. "Where are the gifts I sent her? Why is it that *you* provided her clothing?"

"Omega Superior ordered the clothing you sent be stacked neatly away. It will be offered in due time, but right now? She needs familiarity. Morgaine craves a purpose and to show others her worth." Trapped arm hitched so high her shoulder brushed her ear, bruising in her prince's crushing grip, Etaine kept her face composed.

But it was the scent wafting from her collar that failed to support her collected demeanor; the Omega was nervous, and for good reason. Before her was a *furious* Alpha. A Heidron, no less. Capable and angry enough to end her in every way, and she was the one responsible for delivering news that would displease.

"The Nierra took much from her. You won't replace abused pride with fine fabrics and wealth she does not comprehend." Breath hitching as if the pain had reached a threshold she could no longer pretend to ignore, she hissed, "There was more progress here than you recognize."

Lowering his face so Etaine might see his snarling mouth and feel his breath on her face, Simin grumbled, "Doubtful."

Under his grip the woman's arm twitched, her brow furrowing as she tried to maintain composure. "Her hair was uncovered, Heidron. In Morgaine's settlement, women only leave their hair uncovered in the presence of family, intimate friends, and to impress mates."

Golden hair *had* spilled around the shoulders of his pretty kor'yr. There had even been a few small braids worked into all those waves. And she had preened when he'd complimented the dress…

That small bit of knowledge doused Simin's ire. He released the female.

To Etaine's credit, she didn't rub her arm or scamper back. Like the soldier her robes declared she was, she stood her ground and offered more. "She cannot abide raw meat."

The finest meat was always served raw. To cook it would destroy the delicate balance of flavors. "Explain."

"Their livestock carried parasites, and Morgaine's people were never given the technology to sterilize food or water beyond cooking or boiling. That is why your offerings were replaced with plain dishes common to her people. Simple cheese, boiled oats. The look of relief on her face to be served something other than rich dishes spoke to the Omega Superior's judgment."

Slave food.

They were feeding a princess, a woman who would outrank all of them by a ridiculous degree, slave food. And they were in the right. He might not like it, but Simin understood the wisdom here. "And you say this pleased her?"

"As did making the dress. She worked on it all night so she might wear it today." Etaine was obviously impressed under that stoic expression. "I wish half my team was as focused as your kor'yr."

That Etaine had called Morgaine *his kor'yr* earned

her a minor pardon in his eyes. Pride thrumming from her slipped phrasing, Simin crossed his arms over his chest. "And what other wisdom has your Omega Superior deigned apply to my female?" More content which each passing moment, he teased, "Are you having her sweep the floors?"

"She is uncomfortable with the concept of slaves and already declared she would clean her cubicle. But do not worry, the Omega Superior will not allow her unconventionality to extend beyond her private room. She will be taught Omari ways."

Simin had researched this woman, her military file, her family, who she preferred to take for lovers. "Nierra Psychological Operations translation team lead. You work under Senior Alpha Bishop Amsqin. Do you enjoy that assignment?"

Etaine hesitated, features pinched as if she antici-pated a threat to her position. "Yes. PSYOP is very fulfilling. Amsqin's team influences enemies' choices, plants ideas in adversaries' heads, alters perceptions and persuades outcomes. I believe our work was the cornerstone of our latest Nierra over-throw. They surrendered with practically no military engagement. And if you're asking if I am the only Omega onboard who speaks Morgaine's language, the answer is yes. All other translators are Beta males."

"Sounds as if I have an expert on hand to help my

mate recover; to lead her transition to this new *position*."

A tick came to her jaw, the tick of an Omega who he knew was tempted to point out that Morgaine was not his mate yet. Not until estrous. Not until claiming marks had been made, and certainly not if she never left these rooms. Or maybe that tick was because Etaine understood exactly what he was not so subtly hinting at. A PSYOP operative knew the fundamentals of encouraging the enemy to do as she wished, to winning them over, to mentally repositioning them, as it were. He outright expected her to employ those skills and manipulate the girl. "Sir."

"I expect you to tell me exactly what my kor'yr requires. I will provide it, not the old woman. And I expect you to correct my mistakes in our communication."

"You want *my* advice on how to woo your female?" Such a thing was unheard of; embarrassing for both parties.

Humiliation was nothing to a lifetime without his mate. "Yes."

"I'll"—gnawing her lip as she considered, Etaine took steps toward the safety of the golden line—"send suggestions when I update today's report."

There would be only one acceptable outcome to this arrangement. Though patient and eager to see her happy, Simin was waging a war. War against an ugly, painful history. War against the women who did not trust him enough to release his mate to him. War against his own expectations. "She'll find her way back to her mate, and should she get lost, you will gently nudge her back onto the path."

Etaine didn't look so sure. Out of his reach, once again in the sanctified space where Simin might not touch her, the Omega translator said what Simin feared the most. "She is very young, sir. Even with constant suggestion, Morgaine might not be ready to mate."

"Then I will wait, and meet with her in this blasted hall for one blessed hour of each day until she is."

20

Simin Gralloch, Heidron of the fleet, had groomed his hair and left it loose instead of bound at the nape. He had dressed in the leathers of a warrior broadcasting his prowess, displaying battle scars and warning all who saw the swath of oiled flesh of his tried and tested skill. Unarmored to show potential combatants he was fearless, he came bearing gifts.

This was how she had first seen him. This was how she should know him, just as he would learn to know her on her odd Nierran terms.

Uncovered hair was a sign of flirtation. Well, his was flowing down his back, combed to a shine by his own hand. Not a single slave had been invited to prepare him. He had bathed himself, prepared himself, and milked his cock three times before their meeting so the damned beast might lie down behind the breechcloth.

Etaine's suggestions had been… terrible. The female was not feminine at all.

What kind of woman would suggest offering flowers? They would only die in a day or two. Flawless rubies though, there were so many things that could be done with precious stones.

In an effort to gain at least a little headway, there was a bunch of wilting petals on the tray, dotted with fat rubies to catch her eye. And in the middle of the offering was what he had spent the morning preparing: a pot of gruel and the burnt nutcake Simin had made himself.

After all, it was the duty of an Alpha to feed his mate, prepare meals to an extent, even hunt fresh meat when near a planet that boasted worthy game. But to bake… to stir and season… this was the work of slaves.

She enjoyed slave work. He would try to please her.

Burnt fingers aside, he was determined to impress the woman standing out of reach, wearing the same white dress.

Though today, the dress boasted a bit more detail than the day before. A collar had been sewn on, the sleeves embellished into gathered folds. Even the skirt's silhouette had gone from a shapeless drape that covered her well-formed legs to something that nipped in at a curved waist.

Morgaine looked less like a woman in a shapeless sack and more like a seamstress displaying her work.

Simin took notice, running his eyes from her hidden toes to her glorious hair, he took his time studying what she presented, keeping his expression light and his smile pleased. He then forced his tongue around her strange words, performing the only phrase he'd learned. "Good afternoon."

It sounded appalling, tripping from his tongue, but blue eyes came alive. Shy smile on her lips, Morgaine repeated the pleasantry.

Hearing her form the words, Simin realized he'd said it wrong, but that was not what mattered. The Omega was impressed with his effort.

"Those are the only words I've learned so far, but I will come each day with something new to surprise you." Far more comfortable conversing in his native tongue, he set the tray of food on the golden line for her to take when she was ready. "I made you something to eat, though I am not nearly as skilled with the preparation of recipes as you seem to be with needle and thread."

She looked down at the tray strewn with flowers and sparkling blood-red stones. Bemused, she refused to step forward. "Etaine explained to me that Omari males serve meals to their wives. On Esin's ship, they tried to feed me often. When it was Esin's turn he brought... I can't even remember what he called it."

Retreating a step back before she might smell the musk of Alpha anger in the air, Simin took a controlled breath. He even managed to speak without grinding his teeth. "Did you enjoy his food?"

Lost in her thoughts, Morgaine failed to notice his shift in mood or his blatant attempts to hide it from her. Instead she stared down at the tray with its yellowing flower petals and simple fare. "I never tried it. I couldn't eat after the caning. Or if I did, I don't remember. Nothing there tasted good because everything they served me had been stolen from my settlement. The women here call me Nierra, but my people were nothing like those men."

He could work with this line of information, lead her to pleasant things. Crouching down so he might sit upon the floor and cross his legs, Simin grew casual, smiling as he asked, "I can't make any promises that your lunch will taste good. Fairly certain I burned your cake, but after you eat some, take pity on a poor man and tell me what I did wrong. Tastes like burnt nuts to me. Believe it or not, that was the better of three. The rest were ejected straight into space."

She'd gone from wide-eyed shock to see the male

sprawl on the floor, to trying to bite back a laugh at his foolishness. "I'm sure the inside is just fine."

"So you're saying it's not supposed to be charred on the outside…" Rubbing his jaw, he gave her a playfully pained look. "Don't spare my feelings, I can take the truth."

At that she did let a little snort of laughter free and cracked a grin. "I have not met a man yet who could."

Hand to his heart, insulted grimace on his face, he declared, "You wound me."

He got an honest laugh out of her before Morgaine's hands fisted in her skirts and she began to nervously chew her lip.

When the Omega stood, struck with indecision, Simin urged, "Take the tray. I'm not going to move from this spot. I'll even scoot back if it will make you feel better, though we might have to shout to hear one another if I go much farther."

Slowly inching forward, Morgaine made a grab for the tray, pulling it far enough on her side of the room that even with his great reach, Simin would never have been able to touch her. Mirroring his posture, she set a hip to the floor, legs tucked neatly under her skirt.

Watching as she wielded the provided spoon by the bowl, the Omega sawed off the top of the cake with the handle. Quick work was made of the sides as well, until the unburnt insides of his sorry attempt at baking were carved into a neat rectangle… that actually looked good. Almost edible.

"So that's the trick…"

"Baker's insider secrets. I'm pretty good at burning cooking myself." As she tidied up the plate and cast the burnt edges right atop a particularly large ruby, Morgaine explained. "My mother was the great cook."

"Was?"

A golden head shook, Morgaine correcting herself. "Is."

"You must miss her a great deal."

Hackles raised on the Omega, playfulness morphing into distrustful sharp edges. "Is this some trick?"

"Tell me what she's like?"

Bitterness bleached her expression into a blank slate of nothing. "She's wonderful."

Leaning back on an elbow, affecting his voice to keep it light, Simin prodded, "And?"

"And I don't want to talk about her with you." The snap was rude, it was loud, and across the room where Omegas lounged, several turned their heads.

Brushing off her temper, ignoring the spying women, Simin rolled a shoulder and teased, "I'm my mother's favorite. All my brothers would disagree, my three sisters would as well, but I'm convinced. You might not realize this, but I'm extremely charming."

Morgaine snorted, Simin grinning.

"My father found her on… oh, what was the name of the planet?" For the life of him he couldn't remember. "Somewhere very cold. She led the opposing army. One look at her and he knew, took her right there on the battlefield amidst some very confused warriors who didn't know if they should cheer on the show or keep trying to kill each other. Deep down, I've always suspected that was her strategy all along. Seduce and destroy. Now she is Empress to all Omari and doting mother to twelve, yes you heard me right, twelve children. Though I will remind you again, that I am the favorite. My father is a hard-ass son of a bitch, but he adores her to an embarrassing degree."

His Omega looked stricken, lashes already brimming with unspilt tears. "He raped her before her people?"

Clearing his throat, Simin eyeballed his nails. "The way Mama tells the story, she ran right for him, knives in hand to tear at his leathers. Had him naked and on his back in three seconds flat. Rode him right there on the battlefield for all to see."

First the girl was horrified, then she was confused, and then it seemed to dawn on her what 'rode' might mean. "You're teasing me."

"Nope." That charming grin was back. "Every word is true, though from the look on our scandalized translator's face, she's never heard how their romance began. Now, twelve children later, I think it's safe to say they are both very pleased with the outcome of that battle."

Reaching down for a crumble of his cake, Morgaine took a bite. Sighing she muttered, "I always wanted brothers and sisters."

Eager to hear more, Simin turned his eyes from his nails to lay them upon the most perfect Omega that ever existed. "You're an only child?"

"Of course. I'm Alpha born. My mother was shunned for carrying me."

What? That made no sense to him in the slightest. "I don't understand."

"Alphas are the enemy. They only come to take what they will. One of them *took* her and it was considered unforgivable by my neighbors." Tossing her hair over her shoulder to open the pot of gruel and dig in, Morgaine added. "Esin's ship discovered who my father was while I was in their prison. They executed him."

"You speak of something horrible so lightly, yet I can sense deep sadness between your words. I'm sorry that happened to her, and I'm sorry it happened to you." He meant every word, knowing that someday she would learn more about Omari culture and hate him for their ways with conquered women. But today was not that day. Today, she looked up, mouth full of the food he had made for her, and met his eyes.

This was the moment he had been waiting for. Far from the dividing line, he made his goodbyes and climbed to his feet, purposefully cutting their time short. "I must leave now, sweet Morgaine. My apologies. Please enjoy my gifts."

With her mouth full, she could not reply.

21

Morgaine wanted to pretend these compulsory meetings were tedious, but over the last few weeks they had become the best part of her day. Though it was still hard to look at the Alpha when he walked in, he moved slowly, as if not to scare her.

Or did he move at a snail's pace to show of all that shiny skin to best advantage? She was beginning to suspect it was the latter. The giant lounged on his side, leg out, knee bent, exactly how he had lounged next to her in the sleeping pit before, after, and between bouts of sex. He licked his lips just like that after he had tasted her in places proper women didn't speak of.

Why did he have to arrive practically naked?

A leather loincloth around one's hips was *not*

clothes. Heck, he'd had more on the first time she'd seen him on Esin's awful ship. Yet day after day, Simin marched in with his chest gleaming and his hair a sleek waterfall of black pouring down his back. More than once he'd caught her staring, but who *wouldn't* stare?

Diligent, she'd take his tray, keep her eyes on the food, and relax over time into playful conversation. He was a complete goof, purposefully goading her into laughter at every chance.

Nothing like Esin with his unsettling stares or Uriel's demand for obedience. Simin never demanded *anything*, though he did ask for much.

First, he'd asked her to take the tray straight from his hands so he wouldn't drop the ugly fur hanging over his arm. They had met a handful of days at that point, and he had tried nothing untoward beyond a few bawdy jokes that were funny enough to earn a stifled snort. But to come close enough to the line with him standing right there... It had taken him a good few minutes to coax her to reach out her hands just to take the tray. When she'd done it, she yanked it back, almost tripping on her feet to step out of his reach, and spilled a canister of water all over the flowers and sparkly rocks sprinkled around the dishes.

To say she'd felt incredibly foolish was an understatement. And Simin? He'd looked flat out alarmed. "I wasn't going to try to grab you."

She'd sat down on her rump, plopped the tray on the floor, and put her head in her hands. It wasn't tears that came; it was a feeling of failure.

Taking himself several hasty steps back, the Alpha asked, "Are you okay? Should I leave?"

Even Etaine, who always stood as their translator, broke protocol and stepped forward. "Give yourself a moment, Morgaine. Take a deep breath."

Unable to lift her head from her hands, rubbing at her scalp as if that might stop this fugitive panic and make her normal again, Morgaine whispered, "I've ruined his food."

The woman teased, "It probably tasted terrible to begin with."

A slight chuckle and the tightness in her chest began to ease. "He must think I'm a complete lunatic."

"Does it matter what he thinks?"

Yes. It did matter. He'd been polite, brought her food every day that he had made himself, and she had grabbed at it like an ungrateful crazy person. It mattered because he had not been trying to trick her. He had been trying to share.

Simin was not Esin. Nor was he Uriel. He was the man the others had given her to.

Her head felt as if it weighed more than a boulder, but Morgaine lifted her chin so she might at least look at the person she had offended. "I'm sorry I spoiled your effort."

Etaine translated and the man shook his head. "I should not have pressed you to take the tray." Holding out the fur slung over his arm, the same fur he had used to cover her with when he'd taken her into his possession, Simin said, "I thought you might want something more comfortable to sit on than the floor."

Uncurling her legs, forcing herself to stand, Morgaine approached the golden line and held out trembling hands. Unable to make herself speak, she swallowed, felt the blood drain from her face, and waited.

When the Alpha approached to give it to her, he did so slowly, laying the fur across her arms and backing off without so much as a single touch on her skin.

It was softer than she remembered, pliable and silken. But just as ugly. Hideous even.

She hadn't been able to eat that day, nor had she been capable of much conversation, but they had sat across from one another in easy silence. Every night since, she'd slept wrapped in that animal pelt, and every afternoon, she brought it to their meetings to sit upon.

And every damn day since, she made herself step forward and take the tray from him. Though it had taken at least a week before she'd been able to meet his eyes while doing it.

The smile he had given her... it put a little flip in her belly.

She'd even forgotten to back away once she'd had it in her hand. Morgaine just stood there, staring up at him.

Way up. He was extremely tall. Many times larger than her. And smiling as if he was the happiest man in the world just to stand there and hand her a tray.

She had not noticed how loud he purred until it saturated sweet words. "You look lovely today."

Heavily accented but recognizable, he'd complimented her in her language. Morgaine had blushed bright red as if this were a courting man outside her cottage bearing flowers and a gift of smoked sweet meat. "Thank you."

Then came the teasing "Aren't you going to tell me I look pretty too?"

Giggling, *giggling*, Morgaine stepped back, tray secure in her hands, and went to her fur. "If you're trying to be pretty, I'll gladly sew you a dress. I'm not sure how you keep warm as it is."

"I would gladly have you keep me warm, any way you choose."

When she looked up, she found such heat in his eyes. Longing, hunger, desire, adoration. He looked at her just as he had that first time, only seeing it now didn't send her heart thumping in fear. Nor did his impossibly deep voice. What had at first sounded like two mountains scraping together now reminded her more of a rumbling sea. Soothing, constant, even warm as he changed the subject and talked to her about…

What had he been talking about?

Several times she'd lost track, watching the subtle movements of his body, or the way the light might play off his chest. Lost in thought, Morgaine muttered, "Omega Superior told me I didn't have to meet with you anymore if I did not want to… that I never have to cross the tiled line on the floor or leave these rooms… but I have come to every meeting."

Arms crossed over his chest, head cocked to the side, and paying attention to every last nuance in conversation, Simin stated, "And you don't know why."

"I feel better with you than I do alone in my room." Every word was true. Morgaine had struggled with thoughts of why for weeks. She had struggled with the very obvious fact that she was slowly growing to like *him*. "Maybe it's the purr."

Another one of those glorious smiles. "I'll stop purring and you tell me if you still like being near me tomorrow."

Endless hours of introspection… time she had in abundance here… had yielded nothing to solve the riddle. "I thought it was cologne… something you put on your skin. You don't smell like other males."

Seemingly unconcerned, Simin had shrugged into his lounge. A great big, lazy predator smirking as he said, "I won't smell like other men to you."

"That's my point. You don't smell like a man at all." Realizing that her phrasing was slightly offensive, Morgaine amended, "You see, the fur scraps Uriel made me use in the sleeping pit *stank of men.* You smell like…" She stopped herself and bit her lip.

The wry cock of his eyebrow and twist in his lips didn't exactly look appeased. "Like what?"

Unable to resist a coy jab, Morgaine's eyes came alive. "Food. You smell like spice cake." He pulled a face, making her laugh all the harder. "It's a flattering comparison, I promise. At least, if you like spice cake."

A voice like velvet, the Alpha returned, "I've always thought you smelled like sunshine."

Warmth filled her cheeks and made her shy to look at him.

"I have a question for you, Morgaine."

"Yes?"

"Tell me about your dress. Every day I see something new you've added to it."

Even though she couldn't make herself meet his eyes at that moment, she could feel the weight of his gaze. And knew why today of all days he asked. Over the weeks of their courtship, she'd crafted detail into the skirt, used colored thread to embellish the bodice and sleeves. Today there was something special in the sash around her middle.

Simin had noticed right away, his eyes alight when he first saw her. But he had bided his time before pointing out. "You are wearing green."

"I made the dye from the seeds you delivered. There was enough so I might make the other Omegas a gift. This"—she began to untie the sash died the exact shade of the Heidron's house colors—"I thought *you* might like."

Just as he had offered the fur, Morgaine held out the strip of cloth.

The Alpha looked at it with a sigh, still lounging. "I cannot reach it, kor'yr."

Cautious, she took a step, her foot landing closer to the golden line than she'd ever dared. Outstretched her arm fully, but still he did not raise his hand.

Simin waited for her to come to him.

"If I cross, I'm no longer safe."

"You're always safe with me." Patient, determined, he tried to cast a new light on what they had shared. "I would only hurt you for your pleasure. I only bite so you know I'm yours."

The words sent a chill over growing gooseflesh, Morgaine's eyes on the male's bared chest. The closer she crept, the more obvious his effect on her became.

It was not just the way she inhaled deeply through her nose, it was her eyes. The blue was disappearing, being eaten up by a black pupil. "I'm not ready…"

There was a buzzing between her thighs, and he had not so much as laid a hand on her in weeks. As if he knew, the man drew in a deep breath, fought a groan. "Your estrous will arrive soon…"

Finding that she'd taken another step, that one whole foot was over the line, Morgaine blinked. Heart beating fast, the *whoosh* of blood in her ears almost louder than his purr, she said, "That is what they have told me."

Voice low and suggestive, the lazing Alpha tried to coax her nearer. "What else have they told you?"

"That my first estrous might be difficult." Unblinking, she met his gaze, completely enraptured. "But I'm not afraid of the pain. I've felt it so many times." Another step, the golden line behind her now. "I'm afraid of you."

"I don't think you are afraid of me at all." A gentle curl to his lips, a deeper purr was offered. When she edged even closer, he teased. "If you hold my hand now, you'll see that I can be a lamb."

Near enough to touch, the great, lounging male moved slowly as if to take the green sash, but instead, ran the back of his fingers up her arm. The Omega let out a breath, closing her eyes on a hum.

He dared to touch her loose hair, to tease the

tendrils between his fingers. "And if you let me kiss you now, you'll find that I do taste like spice cake—which I suspect you enjoy very much."

The smell of slick was abundant and rich, wafting from the layers of Morgaine's skirts. Breathless, she murmured, "You brought me here because you knew I was unhappy. You brought me here to this place where I feel safe, a place where you cannot take me away without my permission… and I want you to know that I am grateful."

But he *could* take her away, because she had fully stepped over the golden line. But he didn't do more than kneel at her feet and lightly play with her hair. "Then will you come home?"

In that moment, Morgaine was thoroughly tempted, licking her lips as if imagining licking the expanse of chest that—even with him kneeling—was close enough to kiss. When her eyes traveled downward to find the clear outline of his hard cock behind the leathers, she whimpered. It was not the whimper of fear.

"Please, kor'yr, come home. You don't need estrous as an excuse to be cared for."

Not yet. Laying the green sash over his shoulder, Morgaine asked her final question for the day. "Simin, tell me one thing the Omegas have yet to share. What does kor'yr mean?"

It was the first time she had spoken his name. The

first time she had willingly touched him. The first time she had almost wished he'd carry her off and take the choice away.

Instead he spoke, eyes wide and full of love. "It means soulmate."

22

———

When a chime summoned him in the middle of another sleepless night, Simin knew that this was the defining moment. Estrous had come.

For over a month, he had affected a cool demeanor in front of the female his body and spirit already counted as his, fought to keep things light and easy so Morgaine could grow confident.

All the while imagining how hard he'd fuck her on the floor, right there in front of the translator and all the women gathering in the room behind her to spy. It was impossible to keep his thoughts innocent. Not with the way he'd trained her to look at him.

Not when her skirts—and whatever she had wrapped around her hips under them—couldn't hide the tantalizing aroma of fresh slick.

Her body was begging to be penetrated, satisfied, and knotted.

The last week, her pupils had blown from nothing more than a covert stroke of her fingertip when she bravely took the tray. If Etaine was doing as she'd been ordered, the Omega translator had also been whispering in her ear, guiding her to find favor in him.

And if she hadn't, then biology had done the work.

Morgaine desired him. His sweet kor'yr just needed to reconcile her physical attraction with her mental hesitations. Every meeting was a war against what might as well be considered scrupulous virginity. The more Simin had read about her people, the more he understood.

She required so much more than wooing.

She needed a spiritual conqueror and a physical presence between her thighs. And by the higher power, he had taken on that mantle with a vengeance. Sweet words, laughter, food made by hand and seasoned with fresh come.

Dribbled on her porridge, covertly rubbed over sticky fresh fruits, sweetening her tea. The more he provided the hidden ingredient, the more she seemed to enjoy his cooking... and the closer she came to estrous.

A steady diet of her future mate.

If Etaine had noticed the particular aroma, the translator had never so much as blinked an eye. Nor had he received any form of reprimand from the Omega Superior. The females might have offered Morgaine sanctuary, but in reality, it was in their best interests to maintain a sense of alliance with their Heidron. After all, his men kept them safe from foreign males who would happily enslave and rape them.

His soldiers mated them when they required attention.

Provided them food and comforts—even allowing those who refused to submit to a pair-bond, to choose a life of seclusion.

No, he'd respected their rules, and to keep the balance between the dynamics, he expected his mate returned. No matter the cost.

Omega Sector had taken great care of her. Had prepared her to submit to him more than the young woman might realize.

And only him.

Simin would have her on her hands and knees, ceremoniously presenting her slick flooded cunt and begging for his teeth to pierce her skin. And she would believe it had all been her choice.

Choice mattered to her, even if she never really had one at all. This was not a war the Heidron was ever willing to lose.

And now he was being summoned to go to her… to a female struggling through her first estrous.

A female he was going to keep waiting.

Rolling onto his back amidst the nest he would soon share with her, Simin let his eyes rest on the rut-swollen cock that had dripped beaded pearls of wasted sperm constantly for weeks. He smiled. Even now a fat droplet grew atop the slitted head of his crown, the tiny amount of fluid expanding with each beat of his heart. Watching that pearl grow, waiting to feel it run down his throbbing shaft, he imagined the velvet brush of a feminine tongue lapping up all he offered.

That first rush of come burst forth without so much as a single touch, a spray of scented rain falling to splatter clenched abs.

Hand smearing globs of white, he rubbed his spend on every part of flesh that would be level with her nose.

Before he so much as set a toe into Omega Sector, he would be coated in a tempting display. He would make it impossible for her to refuse.

Fisting the neglected knot that pulsated at the base of his member, he ran a measured stroke over heated flesh in a mimicry of slow sex. Down went that tight fist, another string of come shooting from straining cock to paint the hard muscles of his chest.

Everything had been prepared. His rooms cleaned, his bedding fresh for her to nest. She had never made one before, Etaine's report on that particular fact leaving Simin with no idea of his kor'yr's preferences.

So he had every last item a nesting Omega might want, ready and waiting. A great deal of food had been stored to fortify him through the awaiting bliss. He would be potent for her.

Of course, Morgaine would dine only on fresh cock and be fed bellyful after bellyful of slick-laced semen. She would be drunk on him, begging for his knot to plug her sweet slit. Howling for her Alpha's fluids, his touch, his attention.

He knew what to do to see her satiated and happy. Over the years, Simin had been with many Omegas during estrous. There was a chance even their aloof translator had tasted his cock—not that he remembered a single one of them when it was over. Because none of them had been *her*.

And Morgaine would be in their nest, saturated both inside and out with her mate.

Teasing the base of his cock, under the unsatisfied knot, Simin wrung out a fresh orgasm, and then another, and then another. He bled his sack until there was not so much as a spurt offered in climax.

Until the skin was raw and aching.

It was only fair that he suffer just as she did.

And still he kept her waiting.

An hour passed. Two.

A great deal of water was swallowed, tasteless food shoved down his throat as he gave his body back the nutrients it would require to feed her.

The chime came again, and he gave in to the overwhelming need to go to her.

But first…

Still hard, there was hardly a need to even stroke the inflamed cock bouncing between his legs. Starving for his kor'yr, all it took was imagining their life, the sweet moments they would share, and he was erupting all over again. Milking his knot with a bruising grip, Simin stole every last drop of creamy new seed his sack might make, painted his body with it, even rubbed a taste over his lips so that should he coax a kiss from her, it would be done.

And she would beg to submit.

Just as she should…

THIS WAS unlike the familiar pain Morgaine had been plagued with back at the settlement. Yes, there were shooting cramps that stole her breath and left her sweating, but they didn't hurt so much as gnaw at her. Between her legs was a swamp of angry shocks and leaking need.

Empty, she was so empty.

Confined in her cubicle, she paced, arranged the fur on her bedding, moved it again. Over and over, all the while feeling as if none of this would do.

Where was the necessary pit full of soft things that

must be arranged to ease the sting on her skin? Where was the man who might purr and lessen the tension that kept her teeth clacking together?

It was as if she could already taste spice cake on her tongue.

To just see him, to hear his voice, would ease the consuming need and refresh her. But over and over she had been told he could not come.

Why?

Sobbing at the injustice of it, unsure if she burned with fever or was chilled by the shards of ice traveling through her veins, Morgaine pled with Etaine to ease her *discomfort*.

"There is no medicine for this. Your body will have its way," the woman had said, tired from being woken in the middle of the night. "You either wait out your heat, or ask an Alpha to break it for you."

Tearing at her hair, tempted to throw back her head and howl out her frustration, Morgaine snapped. "The only Alpha I know on this ship refuses to come speak to me!"

"Our Heidron commands this fleet. It might not be that he refuses so much as he is engaged in his duties." Watching how Morgaine picked at the fur clutched closely to her chest, the translator offered, "He courts no other. You have no rival to fear warming his nest. He will come."

Rival?

The thought that Simin might speak to another female as he spoke to her, that he might bring her food, and soft words, had the oddest effect. First rage, then a great cramping sweep of sticky slick that waved from her womb and splattered the floor.

Too absorbed by churning sensation to even be embarrassed, Morgaine glared at the puddle.

Thighs slipping against one another, she succumbed to the need for some form of pressure. Pressing her fist against her mound, trying to catch up the spilling slick in her night garment before more was wasted on the floor, she asked again for her friend. "I just need to hear his purr."

"That's not what you need, Morgaine." Averting her eyes, Etaine explained, "You are almost through transition. Soon, all you'll need is sexual stimulation. Remember what we talked about. Omegas who refuse to mate during estrous must manually handle the urges."

She had been provided with an embarrassingly large, male shaped… tool. It sat under her cot where she'd stashed it the same day the Omega Superior had brought it to her. But it would be cold and lifeless.

A fake organ would not pulsate the way she remembered when Simin laid her down on his furs and silks. It wouldn't fill her with scented cream.

Stomach rumbling, Morgaine began to suck at the tips of her fingers.

Hungry.

But he *always* brought her food. Simin wouldn't forget, right? He would come with something and her mouth was watering just imagining a sweet burst of flavor on her tongue.

A chime rang, snapping her from sultry memory into agitation. "What is that?"

Relief was palpable in Etaine's sigh. "Your kor'yr has arrived."

It never crossed her mind to pull a dress over her shift, to cover her bare feet or recognize that her skirt was saturated. Morgaine fled her room, padding down the hall and across the grand foyer to find that *he had come* at last.

But there was no tray to slake her hunger, no tea to wet her tongue. Near tears, she stopped short and stared wide-eyed.

Simin was dressed.

Offended that so grand a chest had been hidden from her sight, Morgaine refused to look at him.

Winded from the sprint, Etaine arrived on her heels just in time to translate Simin's greeting. "It's late, kor'yr. The Omegas called for me to come to you. Do you have need of me?"

The depth of his voice worked upon her, leading the Omega to grimace. A cramp unlike the others stole her breath and almost sent her sprawling. She had been so wrong. His presence was not a comfort, it only increased the pain.

And now it was *real* pain

"I thought seeing you would help, but"—a rolling cramp stole her breath—"you don't purr!"

At her snappish complaint, he gave her exactly what she'd demanded. Vivid and resonant, Simin gave her a purr unlike any she'd heard before. He let it slip into his words, flavoring the air with promise as he said, "Anything you desire I will give it to you."

Sinking to her knees, the strength fled her body. Frustrated tears falling over red cheeks, she braved another look at him. "I am hungry, but you have brought no food."

A gentle smile on his lips, Simin toed the line, as near to her as he could possibly get. "If you were to eat now, you'd be sick, my love."

"I'm in pain…" Yet all she could do was stare where his trousers tented and grew wet with something that promised to take all the hurts away.

"You are on the cusp of transition into full heat. At this stage, females seek seclusion to prepare their nests. Male presence is… for later." The bulge in his pants bobbed, and Morgaine would swear behind the clinging fabric she could see it throb when he offered, "Shall I leave?"

"NO!" She wasn't commanding, Morgaine was begging. "Just purr, okay. Please purr until this stops."

Black hair dripping forward when he crouched to meet her eyes, Simin shook his head. "It would not be wise to keep me here if you've chosen to be alone through this. Soon you'll reach a point where estrous will take away your choice. You must decide, my beautiful Morgaine."

Nostrils flaring, the Omega began to sniff in his direction and paw the ground to drag herself closer. Practically drooling, she ran her nose up his cloth-covered knee and put her face right to the damp spot at his crotch. Whining, hardly able to form words, she slurred, "Help me."

"Morgaine!"

Startled, a sting in her scalp where the rutting Alpha had gathered her hair, she was made to look up.

Heidron Simin Gralloch's eyes were fiery, his mouth in a firm line as he snarled, "I want you to give yourself to my care because you trust me. I want Morgaine to choose me, not her estrous."

Mindlessly, Morgaine bent back in his touch, the zings along her scalp the furthest thing from pain.

I would only hurt you for your pleasure.

She set her teeth to his wrist.

I only bite so you know I'm yours.

In the blink of an eye, the world felt reborn.

The translator, groggy and half-dressed, stood by as she always did. It was to her Simin pleaded. "Her eyes are fully blown." Morgaine did not understand the fastenings of his unusual clothing, her little fingers fumbling with the layers in an attempt to break free the pulsing organ inside. "You have to pull her off of me. I cannot do it! I will not take her without her word."

Etaine did not answer him. Still as a statue, she watched the couple war with themselves.

The buckle snapped and a happy chirp passed plump lips. Hand closing on something warm, something that could *feed* her, Morgaine smiled.

"I was wrong in this, Morgaine. I should not have made you wait! I want you more than anything, more than any kingdom or ship, but it is a cheap victory this way." Tormented, Simin shook with the effort to hold her back. "Your first estrous is special." He could barely breathe, conquered by one small female. "It's not to be wasted. If you are not truly ready, I can wait for the next one. By then you will understand some of what I say."

He would not let her taste him with her lips, so Morgaine reached out her hands. Smearing the slippery offering glistening on his flared crown, she brought her fingers to her tongue and began to noisily suck them clean as she said. "You would leave me in pain? I'm empty; there is no nest here for me. Take me to yours. Fill me… hurt me for my pleasure like you promised."

"I don't want to hurt you. I want to love you."

Morgaine was ready to make her own conquest. This trembling male may have conquered planets, might be a great warrior of rank, but one Omega was destroying him piece by piece. "I know you love me."

That simple acknowledgment, and Simin spurt. Gobs of aromatic temptation landed on Morgaine's face, collected by greedy fingers. "If I take you to our rooms, you won't leave them unbonded again. You will be mine in every possible way forever."

Desire, lust, hunger, she was all these things—temptation of the slyest succubus as her pink tongue darted out to gather his fluid from the corner of her mouth. "Will you bite me?"

"Oh Gods!" The roar came from him as he grabbed her and slammed his lips to hers. Instinct told her he'd rush her from that open place and hide her away in his nest. There would be his delicious scent; there she would be cared for.

There could he fuck her mindless in every way she needed all the days of her estrous so she never had to feel the pain again.

Etaine made no move to stop her prince as Simin stole the feral foreigner away from their enclave. Rushing through the halls of his warship, his female caught up in one of his arms, he struck out at any male foolish enough to dare enter his path.

Once back in rooms she had not seen in weeks, the door was barred, shutting all pursuing Alphas away.

There would be no changing of her mind. This he explained in a rip of her clothing. This he described by forcing her to her knees so he might feed her the fat head of his cock.

Liquid bliss splashed her tongue. Morgaine desperately sucked his dripping organ for more. The male's intentions were sealed with a roar.

There would be no refusal, he'd snarled. He'd waited long enough, been patient, and all his frustration he would take out on her flesh.

Yes, he would hurt her.

The proclamation brought a rush of slick to pour down her thighs.

His kor'yr he threw into the unmade nest, tearing his coverings away. Falling atop her splayed body, brutal thighs forced her to part for him. Hissing at the sting, Morgaine's struggles were silenced with a single growl, one that left her cunt offering a river of slick.

He would feed on it later, he swore, after she had been made to endure the strength of the mate she had denied for so long. Without so much as a sweet kiss or a pet across her breasts, Simin glossed his cock in her copious slick and penetrated deep with a single, violent thrust.

Bodies collided, subdued estrous-high Omega keening out a cry for mercy

Pumping with a fervor that pushed her body across

the tangled nest, Simin withdrew, yanked her bodily back, and abused her cunt exactly how an Alpha should.

Without Etaine, words were gibberish. If she told him to stop, he'd never know. If she demanded more, there was no way to ask.

This was trust.

He couldn't be rough enough that first mating. His cock couldn't stretch the sting away no matter how hard he brutalized her. Even huge and bursting with semen, it was not enough.

So she dug in her nails and screamed.

There was no release until the knob of flesh began to expand where she ached. He grew inside her, cock kicking out ropes of boiling lava that seared her beautifully and churned behind the growing plug of flesh.

Toes curled when that pulsating mass hit a tender spot that bent screams into a song. Sobbing, she dug her heels into his thighs and tried to angle away from so much feeling. But Simin would not allow such a thing.

He pinned her under his full weight and rocked his hips until the shards of glass in her veins blasted outward. Explosive pain became perfect pleasure.

As it burned away a portion of her madness, as the male knotting her continued to spill, Morgaine lost the fight.

Subdued, she blinked up as if finally realizing

where she was. The sweaty face of the male still rocking his knot-locked hips hovered over her, Simin's lips in a snarl.

He was lost to his rut, blind to anything but his need to breed and subdue. Against the round of her bottom she felt his sack draw up right before another spurt of silken semen flooded her belly and soothed her ache.

It was almost too much. Before she spiraled back into a mindless animal, Morgaine put her hand to his cheek and began to speak.

IGNORING all alien gibberish falling from her lips, Simin ravaged. A lesser Alpha might not have had the experience to know that one could still fuck with a knot in place. There was no need to be still and wait, to allow nature to dictate how much he might spurt and when.

The first knot was mighty, but his aching cock was still hard and eager to fill the slip of her walls even as she held his cock in a vise. When she refused to quiet, he took her by the hair, pinned her knee to her ear, and bent the female so her pelvis was angled perfectly for his needs.

"You asked to come here. You submitted!"

Forcing his girth as deep as flesh and bone would

allow, he swallowed her gasp and mashed his pelvis against her clit.

Another glorious release gathered in the base of his spine, drawing his sack up tight just as a fresh wave of come exploded inside his feral Omega.

Beneath him was perfection: a blissed-out, estrous-high Omega whose cunt milked his knot of every last drop her greedy pussy might take.

Delicate hands stroked his cheek, the light trill of a female purr humming between sounds that were almost familiar. Let her talk her words, there was nothing she could say at this point to change things.

"I trust you."

Simin had never heard those Nierran words side by side, but he knew them from study and playful banter.

Roaring on the end of another almost brutal climax, lips pulled back from his teeth.

"You won't hurt me."

Let her believe that if she would. Once he'd worked this pretty female into the ultimate frenzy, he'd rip a hole into her very soul and tie them together. She would never be able to hide from his power, his influence, or his lust.

He would own her.

Just as much as she would own him.

"You love me."

Powers that be, he did! The sweet smelling feral

bearing all his punishing weight was the *reason* he breathed. High on the very feel of her, Simin rocked their bodies and ground her down against saturated cushions.

Looking down to black eyes shining with love as if she'd understood his words, Simin snarled, "Never doubt it, kor'yr. I love you down to the makings of our shared soul."

She did not smell of fear, nor did her voice shake with indecision. A clever tongue formed her first demand in his language. "Again."

Forever.

He would gladly fuck her until time itself ended.

23

In his eyes, his kor'yr was flawless in her heat. In two days, Simin taught his estrous-high mate how to beg for filthy things in his language, rewarding the insatiable sexual deviant with long laps of his tongue on her leaking cunt—with or without her compliance.

What her body craved was seed: flooding her womb, massaged into her skin, and poured down her throat when she'd grown hoarse from crying out his name. But what her spirit craved was intimacy; best fulfilled with hours of delicate attention to the flesh swollen with need.

She might not always want it, but it was the only way to coax his feral darling to rest.

Legs pinned open, pretty pink pussy dripping with their mutual pleasure just for him to devour, Simin spoiled her. And while he serviced her clit with practiced swipes of his tongue, he would rub the dripping remnants of his spend into sweet hips that would ache when the pain-blinding chemicals of estrous faded.

Already she was bruised. Thinner from two days with nothing in her belly but slick-laced come. When her heat was finally broken, his Morgaine would require days of gentle care and the loving purr of a mate who would lay down his life for her.

He'd never desired to tend a female after the sexual high had faded. All the others had been sent back to Omega Sector to be tended by their own kind.

Some had begged for more, crushed that he had not been tempted to claim them in the heat of the moment. But how could he? Simin had known his kor'yr waited.

And here she was, arching up under him and riding his cock like a fucking goddess.

How he loved her.

The pinnacle of his rut and her heat was on the horizon, the moment where he could set his teeth to her flesh and bite down for more than just stinging pleasure. Already he felt his soul swishing through his physical form, as if ready to reach out and brush its other half.

He wanted her first estrous, their *bonding* estrous, to be perfect.

The choice of *where* to bite…

When an Omega was pair-bonded by force, the mark was often in the shoulder. It was an easy place to reach when knotted and pinning a struggling woman. The arm was considered inelegant, used by sloppy Alphas desperate to seal the connection when a flailing Omega could not be properly subdued. Simin wanted something more for Morgaine.

He wanted to scar her in a place she could be proud of.

Taking her hips in hand, Simin rolled to his back and set the woman stuffed full of his cock into a position they had yet to explore.

Pupils blown, the Omega blinked down at his supine body and frowned. Hands planted on his abs, she seemed unhappy with this change of circumstance, until she slid forward and the edge of his cock hit a place in her only available from this angle.

An animal grunt, and she fearlessly tossed back wild, golden locks and rode him with abandon.

Tits high, nipples hard as fucking diamonds… Simin would never get enough of the view.

Half-lidded eyes met his.

Lips caught up in a lascivious grin, he trailed his fingers between her breasts, purring, "I would have done anything to have you this way. Killed anyone, forsaken my name…"

A pleased sound came from the girl who could not know of what he spoke.

"I know I'm older, that I lack the beauty of my brothers, or the righteousness of a male worthy of you. It matters not. In a few moments I'm going to steal back the missing half of my spirit and give you what I have carried in my chest from birth. You'll have my heart. I'll have your soul."

The thrum of a building climax sparked up Simin's spine, sending him to buck upward and almost unseat his prize. Unwilling to be thrown, Morgaine's cunt seized about his throbbing mass, gripping what was hers as the little Omega rocked her clit against the thumb he offered to appease her.

High on her scent, the warmth of enticing slick dripping down his hips, coating his sack in shined seepage, was delicious. The feel of her skin under his gripping palms right in every way.

Watching her excitement build, the flush creeping over semen-crusted skin, evoked a powerful response from his restless spirit. It was time. Simin's knot began to expand before she was ready, because an Omega could not be bonded unless subdued.

He wanted her wild when he set his teeth to her breast. She had to fight to seal the connection.

Bouncing her up and down his budding knot, pushing the woman past pleasure and into the dangerous territory of delirium, that rush came over him. He sat up, lap full of female. Wrapping his arms around her back he took that long hair in hand, yanked back her head to present those jiggling tits, and set his teeth to the inside of her left breast. Right over her beating heart.

Jaw clamping shut, he set her pleasure into a spinning release that distracted just long enough for her body to register the pain too late.

She struck out, clawing at his back. And so began the budding throb of a pair-bond.

Blood streamed down sweat-slicked skin, bubbling from the corners of his mouth when Simin refused to release her at the first cry. There was an art to the formation of permanent union, one no Alpha had to be taught. Stealing the soul of one's beloved and replacing it with their own was a birth-given right.

The link thrummed to life.

No matter how she wailed in pain, her cunt still rippled and gripped his knot. It still sucked the seed straight from his sack and urged him to offer up more. And this knot—this glorious moment that tied them together for life—he would assure it lasted the remainder of the night.

When she woke, it would be in pain. But as he'd sworn, he would only hurt Morgaine for *her* pleasure. The inevitable tears he would soothe with a soft touch and a dedicated purr. He'd feed his cock down her throat so she wouldn't hunger. He'd lick her sweet cunt until she remembered she could trust him again.

And then, when he broke her heat, he'd tell her that he had her mother on board.

His first gift to his pair-bonded mate.

For he knew what Morgaine desired most in the world and would deny her nothing.

EPILOGUE

There was a murmur like a constant resonate hum within her heart, but it made no sound.

So how could it feel so loud?

Wrapping her in warmth, it washed through sore muscles and exhausted flesh, promising that all was exactly how it should be. For the first time since she'd been taken from her people, Morgaine felt secure.

Loved.

And very, very thirsty.

"Drink." A cup was held to her lips, cool water dribbled into her mouth until she swallowed and sighed.

A masculine purr rumbled into her body, in tune with that bizarre thrum. Cracking open an eye, she found that Simin braced her against his shoulder.

Several days' worth of beard shadowed his jaw. He looked drawn, but his eyes were alive with pleasure.

Pressing the cup back to her mouth, a gruff accent sharpening the soft roll of her language. "Drink again."

Helping him manage the cup, she tipped it back and gulped everything offered, a shadowy memory of swallowing great quantities of something else teasing at her thoughts. Suddenly shy, aware she was naked in the confines of soft blankets and appealing pillows, Morgaine remembered.

This was her nest. She had built it while he had pleasured her with his hands and mouth… and cock.

She knew three different ways to say that word in Omari now.

A whoosh of breath, and Morgaine's hand went to her heart. The sudden sharp sting that met her drew out a quick yelp and downward turn of her eyes.

Swollen and ugly, the twin crescents of an animal bite marred her breast.

"Pretty." The male assured when she grew alarmed with the oozing wound. But it was more than his declaration; it was that throbbing whir in her heart. It too said *pretty* without saying anything at all.

This strange, almost suffocating feeling of completion was the promised pair-bond. A link forged between them that could never be broken.

Many of the Omegas who frequented their sacred

sector during the day had spoken to her of the phenomenon. Most waxed on with dreamy eyes while Etaine translated. They loved their bond with their mates, the closeness and the promise of safety.

But a few had guarded comments. A few had been forced.

One absolutely refused to get up and even greet her mate when he'd come to call. Unlike her, she would not so much as approach the golden line. Morgaine was not permitted to ask her questions, and the woman had never approached to so much as say hello.

Then there were those Omegas who'd chosen to reject such a thing, to cut their hair short, and to exist as *simply female*. Women like Etaine.

The connection in her chest rattled as her thoughts turned almost hesitant. It twisted about her fading reluctance and massaged it with feelings of wonder, Simin pressing a kiss to her mouth.

Her weight was laid back upon the nest, the man, *her mate*, crawling over her as he rumbled out words she didn't know between kisses, and words she did.

Love. Mine. Care. Beautiful. Forever.

Wherever she ached, he somehow knew to rub. The bite mark that made her uneasy, he cleansed with soft cloth. Sour smelling unguent was delicately smoothed over every last bruise, and shockingly pressed into her slit by a mischievously grinning

Alpha who pumped his fingers until she cried out in release. And over the course of his careful ministrations, her aches began to subside.

A long bath followed where he washed off all that sticky medicine, cleansed the tangles of her hair until the burnished gold was smooth and soft, and let her nap against his chest as he worked magic down her spine with probing fingers.

When she was clean and dressed in draping robes the women on this ship preferred, he offered her fabric and the items required for sewing, saying, "Make dress," with a genuine smile.

Simin offered food that was warm, cooked through, and seasoned. Food he had not made, but that waited in the dining area of his domicile. Food that was so familiar, Morgaine swallowed it with the worst blend of a broken heart and longing for what could not be.

It was a recipe of her mother's.

Who was far away and in the possession of men like Esin, Uriel, and the commandant. Men who had harmed her and would do so again.

"Kor'yr?"

Blue eyes wet with tears looked up from a perfectly created stew to find her mate brimming with concern. In fact, he looked ill.

Pressing his hand against his chest as if to soothe an incessant twinge, he said her name, stood, and carefully pulled her from her chair. Without Etaine to translate, most of what he whispered into her hair was lost. But it was the tone that mattered.

He sounded sorry.

Shaking her head, trying to communicate that she did not blame him, Morgaine swallowed down her tears.

This was to be her life now, and he had been better to her than any other male. He loved her. She could feel that clearly when the link warmed and cocooned her pain. She would make the best of it.

Large thumbs wiped her tears away, her Alpha cooing until she gave him a crooked smile. But when she went to reclaim her seat and eat the food with no further theatrics, he pulled her in another direction. The dining chamber behind them, he walked her through the front rooms until they neared the exit.

Assuming he was going to take her back to the Omegas because she was sad, Morgaine failed to notice who waited.

"Morgaine?"

It *couldn't* be! "Mama?"

Morgaine was caught up by the woman she loved with her whole heart in a bone-crushing hug.

Pulling back to make sure it was real, sobbing and spilling out her heart, Morgaine asked, "How are you here?"

Excited, her mother carried on, the smile on her

face aglow with all the joy she had in being reunited with her missing child. "For days the sky burned, huge pieces of the Alphas' ships raining down upon us. Just when we thought things couldn't get worse, barbarians invaded. They rounded up everyone as the Alphas arrived. The whole settlement was dragged away amidst the shooting. Our fields burned… animals were left to wander. While I was being herded onto a ship, a woman named Etaine questioned us—*a woman soldier* if you can believe it. When she learned my name, I was separated from the others and brought here." Cupping her daughter's cheeks as if this could not be real, Elizabeta said, "I was told I was to be a slave for a princess."

Morgaine's blood went cold. "Slave?"

"That I was to cook for her and keep her company. And here I find you!" Embraced her again, Elizabeta wept and kissed her daughter's cheek.

Simin watched the exchange, arms crossed over his chest. When his mate turned to look at him, to assess, he nodded and said in her language, "Gift."

"What about my people? Why take them all?"

It was as if he anticipated her scowling brows and downturned lips, Simin coming forward to press a kiss to her forehead. "Etaine explain."

"The female soldier?" Her mother shook her head. "Etaine was taken by the Alphas—the armored ones. She never made it off the planet."

Thank you for reading *THE GOLDEN LINE*! What will become of Etaine? Keep an eye out for the next standalone in this series! Craving more Omegaverse? Download BORN TO BE BOUND for FREE now!

FREE BOOK! Download BORN TO BE BOUND!
"Unapologetically raw and deliciously filthy!"
- NYT Bestselling author Anna Zaires

Sign up for my newsletter.

Join my Fan Group, Addison Cain's Dark Longing's Lounge, for sneak peeks, giveaways, and a whole lot of fun!

Now, please enjoy an extended excerpt of BORN TO BE BOUND...

BORN TO BE BOUND

Alpha's Claim, Book One

She watched him bolt the door with a rod so thick it dwarfed her ankle, trapping her, cornering the Omega for mating. Unsure if Shepherd had heard, she used her feet to scoot away from the male until her back hit the wall, and tried again. "Food... we can't go out... hunted, forced. They're killing us." Her blown pupils looked up at the intimidating male and pleaded for him to understand. "You are *the* Alpha in Thólos, you hold control... we have no one else to ask."

"So you foolishly walked into a room full of feral males to ask for food?" He was mocking her, his eyes mean, even as he grinned.

The horror of the day, the sexual frustration of her heat, made Claire belligerently raise her head and meet his eyes. "If we don't get food, I'm dead anyway."

Seeing the female grimace through another cramping wave, Shepherd growled, an instinctual reaction to a breeding Omega. The noise shot right between her legs, full of the promise of everything she needed. His second, louder grumbled noise sang inside her, and a wave of warm slick drenched the floor below her swollen sex, saturating the air to entice him.

She could not take it. "Please don't make that noise."

"You are fighting your cycle," he grunted low and abrasive, beginning to pace, watching her all the while.

Shaking her head back and forth, Claire began to murmur, "I've lived a life of celibacy."

Celibacy? That was unheard of... a rumored story. Omegas could not fight the urge to mate. That was why the Alphas fought for them and forced a pair-bond to keep them for themselves. The smell alone drove any Alpha into a rut.

He growled again and the muscles of her sex clenched so hard she whined and curled up on the floor.

It was hard enough to make it through estrous locked in a room alone until the cycle broke, but his damn noise and the smell invading past the rotting stickiness of her clothing was breaking her insides apart.

The degrading way he spoke made her open her eyes to see the beast standing still, his massive erection apparent despite layers of clothing. "How long does your heat typically last, Omega?"

Shivering, suddenly loving the sound of that

lyrical rasp, she clenched her fists at her sides instead of beckoning him nearer. "Four days, sometimes a week."

"And you have been through them all in seclusion instead of submitting to an Alpha to break them?"

"Yes."

He was making her angry, furious even, with his stupid questions. Every part of her was screaming out that he should be stroking her and easing the need. *That it was his job*! With her hand still pressed over her nose and mouth, her muffled, broken explanation came as a jumbled, angry rant, Claire hissing, "I choose."

He just laughed, a cruel, coarse sound.

Omegas had become exceptionally rare since the plagues and the following Reformation Wars a century prior. That made them a valuable commodity which Alphas in power took as if it was their due. And in a city brimming with aggressive Alphas like Thólos, she'd been trapped in a life of feigning existence as a Beta just to live unmolested, spent a small fortune on heat-suppressants, and locked herself away with the other few celibates she knew when estrous came. Hidden in plain sight before Shepherd's army sprung out of the Undercroft and the government was slaughtered, their corpses left strung up from the Citadel like trophies.

Claire had been forced into hiding the very next

day, when the unrest inspired the lower echelons of population to challenge for dominance. Where there had been order, suddenly all Thólos knew was anarchy. Those awful men just took any Omega they could find; killing mates and children in order to keep the women—to breed them or fuck until they died.

"What is your name?"

She opened her eyes, elated he was listening. "Claire."

"How many of you are there, little one?"

Trying to focus on a spot on the wall instead of the large male and where his beautiful engorged dick was challenging the zipper of his trousers, she turned her head to where her body craved to nest, staring with hunger at the collection of colorful blankets, pillows —a bed where everything must be saturated by his scent.

An extended growl warned, "You are losing your impressive focus, little one. How many?"

Her voice broke. "Less than a hundred... We lose more every day."

"You have not eaten. You're hungry." It was not a question, but spoken with such a low vibration that his hunger for *her* was apparent.

"Yesss." It was almost a whine. She was so near to pleading, and it wasn't going to be for food.

The prolonged answering growl of the beast compelled a gush of slick to wet her so badly, she was left sitting in a slippery puddle. Doubling over, frustrated and needy, she sobbed, "Please don't make that noise," and immediately the growl changed pitch. Shepherd began to purr for her.

There was something so infinitely soothing in that low rumble that she sighed audibly and did not bolt at his slow, measured approach. She watched him with such attention, her huge, dilated pupils a clear mark that she was so very close to falling completely into estrous.

Even when Shepherd crouched down low, he towered over her, all bulging muscle and musky sweat. She tried to say the words, "*Only instincts...*" but jumbled them so badly their meaning was lost.

Starting with the scarf, he unwound the items that tainted her beautiful pheromones, purring and stroking every time she whimpered or shifted nervously. When he pulled her forward to take away the reeking cloak, her eyes drew level with his confined erection. Claire's uncovered nose sniffed automatically at the place where his trousers bulged. In that moment all she wanted, all that she had ever wanted, was to be fucked, knotted, and bred by that male.

Only instincts...

Shepherd pressed his face to her neck and sucked in a long breath, groaning as his cock jumped and began to leak to please her. He had gone into the rut, there was no changing that fact, and with it came a powerful need to see the female filled with seed, to soothe what was driving her to rub against her hand in such a frenzy.

The words were almost lost in her breath, "You need to lock me in a room for a few days..."

A feral grin spread. "You are locked in a room, little one, with the Alpha who killed ten men and two of his sworn Followers to bring you here." He stroked her hair, petting her because something inside told him his hands could calm her. "It's too late now. Your defiant celibacy is over. Either you submit willingly to me where I will rut you through your heat, or you may leave out that door where my men will, no doubt, mount you in the halls once they smell you."

Read BORN TO BE BOUND now!

ADDISON CAIN

USA TODAY bestselling author and Amazon Top 25 bestselling author, Addison Cain's dark romance and smoldering paranormal suspense will leave you breathless.
Obsessed antiheroes, heroines who stand fierce, heart-wrenching forbidden love, and a hint of violence in a kiss awaits.

For the most current list of exciting titles by Addison Cain, please visit her website: addisoncain.com

facebook.com/AddisonlCain

bookbub.com/authors/addison-cain

goodreads.com/AddisonCain

Que (coming soon)

Cradle of Darkness Series:

Catacombs

Cathedral

The Relic

A Trick of the Light Duet:

A Taste of Shine

A Shot in the Dark

Historical Romance:

Dark Side of the Sun

Horror:

The White Queen

Immaculate

Also Available from NineStar Press

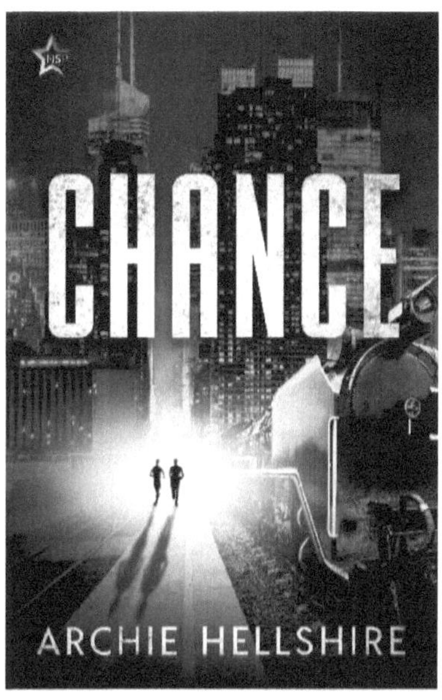

Connect with NineStar Press

Website: NineStarPress.com

Facebook: NineStarPress

Facebook Reader Group: NineStarNiche

Twitter: @ninestarpress

Tumblr: NineStarPress